THOSE SUMMERS AT MOON FARM

Also by Carol Lake:

Rosehill (Portraits from a Midlands Town)
Switchboard Operators
Wendy and her Year of Wonders

Those Summers at Moon Farm

Carol Lake

UNITED WRITERS
Cornwall

UNITED WRITERS PUBLICATIONS LTD
Ailsa, Castle Gate, Penzance, Cornwall.

British Library Cataloguing in Publication Data:
A catalogue record for this book is
available from the British Library.

ISBN 9781852001414

Printed in Great Britain by
United Writers Publications Ltd
Cornwall.

In loving memory of
Doreen Rudge and Joyce and Edmund Cooper
and for Peter Rudge with love.

Acknowledgements

I would like to thank Glynis Greenman and
Peter Rudge, for sharing memories and
anecdotes, and Malcolm Sheppard for his
invaluable help and guidance in the process
of publication.

Author's Comment

Although inspired by real people, this story,
which I call a roundel, is fiction and should
be read as such.

Contents

> *'I have had a most rare vision. I have had a dream, past the wit of man to say what dream it was.'*

Nick Bottom,
A Midsummer Night's Dream
by William Shakespeare.

1

WEDDING

By the time the town clock struck six most of the stallholders in the market square had dismantled the canvas over their stalls. In early summer the sun still poured radiance into the day, and the shadow of a pale moon waited in the heavens, scarcely visible.

In the small market town of St. Edfric's, named after a ninth century Saxon boy whose bones lay in the abbey, the market was held in the square formed by the Cornhall, Woolworths and the flint town hall. Purdy's tea shop and Marks and Spencer made up the quadrangle. A few late shoppers still lingered. The scattering of tourists who came tended to be passing through, or they used St. Edfric's as a base from which to tour the pretty Suffolk villages, but the holiday season proper did not begin until July. St. Edfric had been a nine-year-old Saxon king martyred for his adherence to Christianity, and had no following – there being known little about him – but a general interest in matters Anglo Saxon drew a trickle of visitors each summer. The story of the boy-saint had been grafted on to a much older, much nastier story of the ever-green king hacked to pieces, his head resprouting to confound his enemies; and from Edfric's flowing blood sprang lilies and corn.

At four-thirty, at five o'clock and at six-thirty the small

square was suddenly crowded with people waiting for buses. And after the last bus had departed very little happened. There was a small cinema, a few public houses and a hotel, and a tiny eighteenth century theatre which occasionally opened, usually for enthusiastic amateur productions of old musicals. A snack bar, sport of a late nineteen fifties milk bar, took to opening until eight thirty, did little trade, and resumed six o'clock closing. Certainly these streets were quieter than they had been in the Middle Ages, when in June they were pushing with merchants from the continent, come to haggle for the abbey wool.

Almost an hour later a man walked slowly up the steep hill of Hatter Street, towards the town centre. Few people were in the streets, in spite of the crush of the previous hour. A boy went past on a bicycle. As the town clock in its flint building showed six fifty-nine, the man crossed the market square, remembering the times when he had used to come here regularly to get the weekly supply of groceries, years before.

The bells of the abbey started chiming the hour, and were caught up by the bells of saints Mary, Faith, Peter, James, Ermin and Elfbrigga, the deep chimes of the abbey under them all, St. Edfric's own bells, a flood of sound taking over the streets.

At seven forty-five he was due to meet a train. He thought he might turn into the Green King and have a quick drink. Then on impulse, he changed his mind, and turned back down Hatter Street. He had decided to have a stroll in the Abbey Gardens. There was plenty of time for a drink later. He marvelled that a place with so much activity in the day could so rapidly empty, and in the summer too. An occasional passer-by made their way to the hotel or a car. About to cross the road, he hesitated, stopped, and then continued along the same narrow pavement of the steep street.

Further down, a girl in jeans was smacking at a vending machine. Becoming agitated, she started to thump it. Feeling he needed a diversion, he kept on walking until he reached the girl. His first thought was that such a contraption as a chocolate machine was out of keeping with the town. He was

10

right, and it disappeared at the end of that summer.

'What's the matter – have you lost your money?'

The girl growled, 'Yeh.'

He gave the machine a thump from the top and twisted its knob, but nothing happened.

'The shop's closed,' said the girl semi-bleakly. She had long dark hair and a white blouse with daisies set into it.

'The shop's closed, everywhere's closed. After all, it is seven o'clock you know.' He spoke lightly, teasingly. When he looked at her she looked faintly familiar. But then they all did, all young people resembled one another nowadays.

As she turned recognition appeared in her face immediately, for she had only been interested in extracting the chocolate, and had not at first looked at the man who spoke to her. She recognised him at once. 'Hello,' she said.

'Are you here for the wedding?' he asked then, still not recognising her.

'Oh hell. I forgot it was now. I've just come from the coast, and I was thinking it'd be fun to spend midsummer eve at the abbey while I'm this close.'

'Well there doesn't seem to be much happening here.'

They stood as if stranded, washed up like creatures out of their natural element, on the narrow pavement of the mediaeval street, with the echo of now silent bells hanging in the air about them.

He was seized with a sudden overwhelming need to avoid responsibilities. 'How about a drink?' he suggested.

'Okay,' she replied, with the ungraciousness of youth.

They moved off together, he making for the Green King, as he had previously promised himself, she not having the least idea where she was going.

Moon Farm stands on a road running deep into the East Anglian countryside, in a horizon filled with sky and young corn. Great and small barns and outbuildings are on its left side, among blackberry brambles and lucerne, planted by the farmer to feed stock. On the other side of the house is the

11

overgrown kitchen garden, with its stiff hedge densely packed with dust and spiderwebs, and an appletree which throughout autumn drops large holey cookers into the long grass. Beyond the hedge and ditch, fields of young corn stretch onward, right up to the sky. Behind low hedgerows the fields appear to lie across the road – which is really more like a lane, although it accommodates cars when they do pass. Behind the elm tree and the gate painted with ancient white paint, the front garden has an old roofed well, bound about with ropes of ivy, and clumps of flowering honesty. A jar of their moonpods collected from the previous autumn's garden stands in the bay of the front window.

From under wooden fretwork eaves come bird sounds and movement, and the cry of children floats round the house corners from the back garden.

A woman comes out onto the porch and stands under its fretwork. Her eyes lift to the trees waving about the house. She stands for a moment, looking at nothing, the noise of waving summer trees loud in her ears, throbbing blood coursing through her veins. As she stares she seems part of the triumphant waving and blooming of the summer, whose trees are reflected in her eyes.

'Ch-ch-ch. Ch-ch-ch,' – she calls the cats for their evening meal, then walks halfway up the front path, breathing in the evening, and the smell of her life as it is at this precise moment in time. Her eyes narrow against the evening sunshine, which glances off the leaves of the tree like silver and golden bubbles. Walking to the gate, half rapt, she looks across the fields of corn, silver-green as yet. Her reverie is broken by the muted sound of the telephone. A young voice calls from the house. 'Mother. It's Margaret about the sheets.' The woman hurries back into the house, closing the front door behind her.

In the garden at the back a boy and girl stamp out the last of the burning coals on their midsummer eve bonfire, before going inside to prepare for bed. The fire was a token gesture only, for they had wished for a proper fire to burn into the night. But tomorrow their grown up sister was to be married, and so their bedtime was decreed to be at an earlier time than usual, so they would be fresh for the festivity.

Hazel Marlowe, the children's mother, called them for the third time. She was a fair woman in her mid-forties, with small bones, a stomach round and knotted with having borne children, and slim well-shaped legs which had danced to the music of the Big Bands in her youth. They were now walking into her sitting room.

'That was Margaret on the phone, about the camp beds and the extra bedding. Alan will drop them off tonight,' announced Lynnet.

'Oh good. Then I can get most of the extra beds made up, and the beds downstairs will have to wait,' said Hazel lightly. She never became flustered over domestic arrangements.

This imminent wedding was a source of joy, and also a little trepidation, for her own marriage had led to a divorce ten years previously. Hazel also regarded the arrangements for the wedding as something of a personal triumph. For she had managed to get her ex-husband (although *she* regarded him as still her husband) to agree to foot the bill for the reception and thus, in her eyes, make public acknowledgement of his ties to her and to their children. Hazel was determined that everything would be done properly. By judicious saving and taking thought she would foot the drinks' bill. Brides' fathers gave them away and paid for their reception. It was a generally accepted fact, however old-fashioned such notions were held to be throughout the nineteen-sixties, which had ended the year before.

He had proved slippery at first. He always was where money was concerned. With four more children with his second wife in addition to the four living children he and Hazel had produced, two homes, a cadillac, and a predilection for French brandy, he needed the money he had. He was a science fiction writer and finished a book a year. But his money was his money. He clung to it fiercely, like a principle – particularly where his grown-up children were concerned. As he had made his way in the world, so must they.

'Do you mean to say,' he had barked back down the telephone, 'that I'm supposed to pay through the nose because an adult woman wants to shack up with some man?' He spoke of his daughter Lynnet.

Hazel bounced back, 'Your daughter.' And then what she evidently regarded as a trump card – 'And my father paid for our reception.'

He wasn't listening. 'Anyway, I thought Lynnet's lot didn't believe in marriage. I thought it was a thing of the past, fit only for near-dinosaurs like us,' he said, hoping to play on her generational solidarity.

But Hazel was not to be trifled with on this occasion.

' "Make Love not War",' he quoted desperately. Two summers before Lynnet had painted this slogan, ubiquitous among the young, on the house in Moon Farm kitchen.

But it didn't matter what he said. In her mind this was the chance he had of redeeming the years of what looked to the outside world like neglect.

She unpacked the children's shoes from the catalogue parcel. 'Cross your fingers these will fit. It's too late to send them back now. You'll have to wear your old shoes if they don't fit.'

'But I wanted bar shoes,' wailed Hebe.

Shane came in, from mending his bike. 'Would you make us a pot of tea, dear, to restore us to our senses,' Hazel requested of him. He disappeared unspeaking into the kitchen.

Although she enjoyed coming back home, it usually irritated Lynnet in a minor way, she couldn't say why. Yet coming back, surrendering to her mother's way of doing things, seemed quite different this time. She was pleased to give way to how Hazel ran the house, since she would soon be in charge of her own household, officially as well as unofficially, for she and Jonathan had been living together for six months.

Lynnet erected the ironing board and plugged in the iron, while Hazel poured the tea, then she opened the cupboard door next to the brick fireplace, where freshly washed clothes were put to await ironing. Lynnet then went off to wash her hair, and Hazel began to press trousers. She ironed quietly, taking pleasure in the fresh clothes under her iron. She was pleased, on the whole, at the forthcoming wedding. Jonathan wouldn't have been her exact choice for her daughter, but he was pleasant and steady, and certainly preferable to many of the young men Lynnet had had in tow. Lynnet hadn't lived at home since she was eighteen, only retiring to Moon Farm to recuperate during illnesses or failed love affairs, and at holiday times to show off her young men. Yet there was still something in her situation of the antique kind. Her father was coming to give her away, and here she was on her wedding eve, back at Moon Farm.

The front door knocker rapped quickly, and Shane ushered in a man with his arms full of blankets.

'Ah. Hello. Can't stop. I see you're very busy – how goes it?' This was barely a question, before he rushed on to, 'Have you heard from Rex, is he definitely coming?'

Hazel nodded. The younger children Hebe and Nick said nothing, but pricked up their ears. Rex was their father. The name had a magic effect on all the people in the room.

Margaret Barber put down the telephone receiver and went into the kitchen to make a bedtime milk drink for her eight-year-old.

She had been a close friend of Hazel's ever since her marriage to Alan, twelve years before. Alan Barber's friendship with Rex and Hazel was of even longer duration. As a young unmarried man he had spent many evenings in their company. They had watched him get into and out of involvements with women, until he finally turned up with Margaret.

As merry young married people, the four of them – Rex and Hazel and Alan and Margaret – had shared new gadgets and jokes and bottles of cheap red wine. Every Thursday morning Alan had driven his new wife over to the Marlowes' big Elizabethan cottage, and Hazel and Margaret had done their laundry together in Hazel's new washing machine. Their actual time together, all four of them, was only two years. Yet afterwards it expanded in their memories and seemed much longer, an age, and very golden. When Rex had walked out on

Hazel, leaving her with a schoolgirl daughter, small children and an imminent baby, she turned quite naturally to the Barbers. The two women became closer. As Rex walked out, the Barbers had walked in. The initial situation – Alan the large surrogate infant of Rex and Hazel – had changed into Hazel, the abandoned one, left in the care of Alan and Margaret. Although it often seemed to Hazel that she had been left in charge of two large clueless extra children.

Two or three years younger than Hazel, Margaret had a soft sweet voice and firm ideas about nothing in particular, and an attachment which was still fierce to her old boarding school.

The telephone rang. Margaret stopped stirring her little boy's drink and went to pick up the receiver. The pips went three times, but no one answered. After waiting a few seconds, she put the receiver down. There was only one person likely to ring from a telephone box. In much the same way that Alan and Margaret were critical of Hazel's way of rearing her young, so was she of theirs. This crystallised round her daughter, known for the purpose of face-saving – an activity despised by Hazel as a lie – as her sister. The fact of the girl's existence brought Margaret and Hazel closer together, for they were both women with children who had been deserted by men.

At Moon Farm Hazel sewed a button on Shane's blazer. Lynnet was pressing her wedding dress, fresh from the milkman's wife, who did dressmaking in her spare time. A deal of fuss and frills appealed to neither Lynnet's budget nor her inclination. Headdresses, crystal tiaras, wired waxen flowers, left her cold. Jonathan wanted her to wear white and a veil and to carry red roses. She had yawned at the suggestion. Red roses she felt were like an idea with a heavy frame around it; waxen lilies overpoweringly scented made her think of Victorian graves and death, or of a chastity redolent of its own importance.

'If you've sorted through the old clothes and things you don't want, I can fill up my Oxfam boxes. What about this lovely blouse? Are you sure you don't want it?'

Lynnet shook her head, the wet hair swinging loose. 'I never want to see *that* again.'

'Perhaps Jandy would like it,' mused Hazel, folding the blouse carefully.

'Where is she, anyway?'

'I don't know, I haven't heard from her for ages.'

'I should have thought she might have been asked to this 'ere do,' said Lynnet.

'Oh Lynnet, you know – lots of relations and formality – it isn't really her scene.'

'That's true. Yes, I guess she'll like a wild undergrad party much better, when we get back from the honeymoon.'

'Much more her thing. Besides, we'd got to keep the numbers down,' said Hazel, ever practical. Jandy was Margaret Barber's daughter. She was a couple of years older than Lynnet, and corresponded fitfully with both of them.

'Is everything all right? Is there anything you want to discuss, dear?' Her elder daughter didn't much go in for talking things over, but she wanted to give her the opportunity. As the eldest child, Lynnet had taken the brunt of the divorce. Shane was eight years younger and, as always, had taken it in his stride, cheerfully bestowing his attention on both parents, imperially impartial. The others had been too young to remember the time when their parents were together. But Lynnet, long an only child, was twelve and very resentful. Hazel recalled her perpetual adolescent expression – dark brows knitted together in semipermanent discontent, sentences which often began 'Why *should* I . . ?' And then she found politics. All the shortcomings in her own life were magnified then into the shortcomings of the world. But Hazel and Lynnet had been left together, two forsaken females. Of all the children, only Lynnet lived through that time along with Hazel.

Hazel smiled, as the chestnut leaves waved through the side window and cast lively evening shadows against the sitting room walls. It didn't seem so very long before that Lynnet and Jandy, their long hair swinging and their new transistor radios at full blast on pirate radio stations, had painted this room, sloshing the paint on gaily, laughing and arguing.

'Well – it's just . . . sometimes I've wondered,' said Lynnet, breaking Hazel's reverie, 'I still think of Mark. Quite a lot really.'

For two summers she and Mark had been together, their days filled with love and nonsense. And then he left her. He was blond, with big shoulders and a big vision. His name added lustre to everything for Lynnet. She still spoke of him quite often, in a seemingly casual way. Hazel, though pleased he hadn't been swept under the carpet, was yet avid that her daughter shouldn't tread the path of the dispossessed, she thought her own self-abnegation in the face of the Male quite enough for one family. She didn't think consciously that a woman's ability to throw herself away is her most precious possession and a supreme act of freedom. When Lynnet said, haltingly, 'What if you've given your heart, made your commitment, and it falls through?'

'Then there *is* no commitment,' stressed Hazel fiercely. 'It's null, it's void, it doesn't exist.'

'No. I suppose not.' Hazel took over the pressing of Hebe's dress, and Lynnet escaped upstairs.

In the Green Man, Rex ordered drinks at the bar and the girl went to the cloakroom, and then sorted through coins and put on a record. Last year's hit song whispered through the darkened snug. *'Mmmm mmmm mmmm mmmmm mmmmmmmm, ooooo ooooo ooooo oooooo ooooooooo, Je t'aime Je t'aime . . . '*

'I thought St. Edfric's was too backward, ie forward, to have a junk-box. Unhappily I was wrong,' said Rex, putting glasses on the table and surveying with approval his bejeaned companion, slipping into the seat beside him with newly-combed hair.

Margaret carefully pulled out a mug from the heap of dirty pots on the draining board, put on rubber gloves and hurriedly splashed a hand mop inside and out of it. She always put off washing the pots for as long as she could. Tugging at the rubber, she removed the gloves by rolling them inside out. Anxiously she examined the rash on her finger. It plagued her left hand, so much so that she had to remove her wedding ring, on the suspicion the gold was causing or at least exacerbating the rash.

The Barbers had just celebrated their twelfth wedding anniversary. In their early thirties when they married, Margaret had moved in to share Alan's life on the farm. He farmed for several years, at an increasing loss, and eventually took the decision to sell up. First of all he sold car-insurance. Although reluctant to admit it for some time, he enjoyed this work much more than farming. Urbane yet with a gullibility that appeared almost total, in his new work this quality conspired in his favour. He seemed without an inclination to pursue high-pressured salesmanship and clients trusted him the more because of it. The farm had actually belonged to his father, a general practitioner, and it seemed to Alan that he was at last standing on his own feet, providing for his home and wife and their two small children – the plump-fingered sunny little boy and a wisp of a baby girl.

Margaret was tasting late the pleasures of motherhood. Her hair, which for years had been always recovering from a permanent wave, was caught back, though not very expertly – the ends escaped in all directions at the back – to the amusement and exasperation of her friends. Any doubts she had had about Alan's attitude towards children – as a bachelor he had been a fierce verbal disciplinarian and Hazel's way of rearing her children often appalled him – abated when their own came along, and he proved the fondest of fathers.

Alone in her old bedroom – now taken over by Hebe, but for this wedding week given back to her – Lynnet sat perched on her dressing table stool, looking back at herself in the mirror. The same mirror that had first shown a discontented betrayed twelve-year-old girl glowering back. The room was the same room that had been suddenly hers years before, with its window facing onto a crescent of cornfields, its ceiling sloping down. Hebe's school things were scattered on top of the large bookcase and the bamboo table, just as her own had been.

Hazel had ordered the dressing table and matching bedroom furniture in a fit of fury when Rex left. Together they had shared hardship, and just as he was starting to succeed and make some money he walked out. In an anguished fury, she sold the house in order to settle their many bills, she said. She bought with the proceeds a bedroom suite, in a desperate attempt to have something material, something solid, to show for the years of work and waiting. A bedroom suite was about the most useless item. Perhaps that's why she chose it.

Lynnet, sitting at the dressing table on the eve of her wedding, remembered only that suddenly there was new furniture and nowhere to live, her father was gone, and another baby on the way.

The dressing table still wore its old skirt, with abstract pattern of lime green bars and tomato coloured squares and yellow and black squiggles, belonging so completely to the 1950s. Then it had seemed exciting, Lynnet could remember when the squares and squiggles had seemed like hieroglyphs spelling out a new freedom, gaiety, unrestraint – the shapes swarmed over wallpaper and fabric indicating prosperity after the post-war penny-pinching. It really looked rather shabby now, but Lynnet was fond of it because it had been there a long time and belonged to the dressing table.

She tinkered with the big valentine tucked into the side of the mirror, which she had brought with her. Jonathan had sent it just after they had decided to marry, his small signature neatly penned under the card's extravagant phrases. They had been living together for six months, unknown to Hazel, whose rhetoric was rather more libertarian than her practice, as Lynnet judged. After her first love had walked off Jonathan had picked her up and helped her keep the pieces of her life together. Both of them had been left, part of his entourage, and he and Lynnet had come together quite naturally.

20

She flipped over letters and photographs in a small box, all relics of the other, the first man. She still felt a small knot of grievance, almost physically located in her stomach, she felt he had walked out and left her in the wreckage of their affair. When she and Jonathan had visited her father and Gillian, his second wife, he had inveighed against marriage and said no true man could be satisfied with one woman, it was unnatural. 'I give it five years,' he said helpfully. The idea of this made her fearful, she felt suddenly ill at her stomach, and in order to calm down she started to fold her clothes methodically. Then she put the old letters away. They would never meet again. The prospects for Jonathan's and her own future were bright.

She smoothed her wedding dress, then closed the wardrobe door and thought of tomorrow, when her father would arrive.

In a bedroom of the Angel sat Rex Marlowe with his hands round the belly of a brandy glass, watching his young companion, who sat in a low chair opposite, her palms spread out, her fingers curled upwards, looking back at him.

Alone at last, Hazel had a cigarette. Tomorrow her parents and sisters and many more relations would be here, there would be makeshift beds in practically every room. The other bed in her own room stood made up and ready. She tweaked aside a curtain and swung open the small side window, gazing into the blackness and leaves of the chestnut tree. Stillness.

So. Here she was at another point in her life – the marriage of her first child. She recalled, from years before yet time was irrelevant somehow, the first movings of another life inside herself, and her feelings of disturbance, excitement, resentment. She was being carried forward on the flux into the future. And that future had arrived.

She and Rex had married in that incredible winter of 1945, when there was much shortage of food and many other things, and so much jubilation, the like of which never came again in any of their lifetimes. Rex had just been demobbed from the merchant navy, and they had nothing shared between them. He didn't even have any decent civilian clothes, he had to borrow a suit from his father's younger brother to wear for the marriage. Hazel couldn't remember what she had worn. A two-piece, she thought. Yes, and she remembered the flowers, a corsage of fresh flowers, cripplingly expensive that winter. And – yes, that was right – it came back to her in a rush of memory – she briefly inclined an ear, thinking she heard one of the children. She must have imagined it, there was only stillness – she had worn a hat, a fancy expensive hat that her father had given her. It even had its own hat-box.

When they came to the station all the relations had lined up on the platform to wave them off. She had waved back with her lacey handkerchief, the flowers of her corsage wilting but still making her dizzy with their perfume. And as soon as they had received the last scatter of confetti and were in the train Rex had pulled her into the carriage, he had taken her into his arms and kissed her and then held her away from him and said, 'One moment. Something I've been wanting to do all morning.' And he had lifted her hat very carefully from her head, surveyed its crown, its intricacies of ribbon and veil. Her hair released, she had laughed, and agreed with him it was a silly hat, and kissed him again. And then, as the train started to chug out, he had hurried her out of the carriage into the corridor. As they waved from the door Rex had skimmed the hat out of the window, together they watched it float away down the track, to the astonishment of the assembled line of relations, some of whom supposed it must be an old forgotten custom. From the train they waved, Rex squeezed her tightly as the train picked up speed, and they laughed as they waved their old lives goodbye.

Alone, Hazel gazed into the blackness of the summer night with a smile.

In their room Hebe and Nick had just begun their secret midsummer feast – a grand collation of cheese tarts, rather dry cake saved from teatime, Spotty's dog biscuits, and what Hebe described as 'shamrock sandwiches' – lucerne picked from beyond the big barn and sprinkled with sugar – as well as fizzy lemonade and two sticks of coltsfoot rock.

Two miles away, through the summer dark, the Barbers' dog howled periodically. Margaret, unable to sleep, rubbed at the rash on her finger. Alan tossed and turned, and then stumbled across the bedroom carpet to open a window.

In town in a room in a hotel a girlfriend of Rex's chain-smoked and supposed she ought to curse but couldn't be bothered.

Miles away, through the East Anglian summer night, the bridegroom was tippling with his friends and getting ever so slightly drunk, as everybody knows a bridegroom should do.

At Moon Farm Hazel in her nightclothes was speaking to her mother on the telephone, while Shane mended a light socket.

At midnight on midsummer's eve at Moon Farm only the bride, fortified with a milk drink, was sleeping like a child.

Rex Marlowe felt for his cigarettes in the pocket of his jacket, slung over the back of a chair. At the bedside, in a big glass ashtray she had filled with water, lay a limp white carnation, given out the day before by an itinerate Indian mystical sect, in exchange for a casual donation. She had been reluctant to throw it away. Now he cursed as he had to look for somewhere else to put his ash. These flower children.

These flower children. Flowers in their hair, behind their ears. Any flowers, any flowers but not red poppies. What did these flower children know about the basis of their freedom? He looked between the bed-curtains to the dead limbs cast across the bed, and took a long gasping drag at his cigarette. This sleeping child. By the time he was her age he had killed in the war, had seen friends die, and had a wife and child to support. She had developed from those things called teenagers. Even at fifteen he hadn't been a teenager. He had had to be a man. A young man, maybe – and he cringed at the recollection of his rashness. But still a man, and not a perpetual chrysalis. Hazel was a woman at this age, and yet she was more truly vulnerable than these child-like creatures with long hair and intact ideals.

1965

In the summer afternoons of the mid-sixties the Marlowes had their lunch out on the lawn, and when the children had departed to their various games and Shane and Dale Perkyn had gone off to his bedroom to mess about with potions and chemistry sets, Hazel brought out her cigarettes, Jandy made a pot of tea, and they sat talking together in the sun. All about the garden fat hens picked about, butterflies moved among the buddleia, and the two females sipped and talked.

'Here we are – that's Harry, my first boyfriend.' Hazel handed over a snap of a wiry dark-haired young man, wearing heavy spectacles. 'We were on a hike to Kinder when that was taken. We used to go there quite a lot. When I was a child my parents had taken me to the Mass Trespass in 1932, and Harry was there too, but we didn't know each other then?'

'How long did you go out with him for?'

'Quite a few years. We were both in the movement to defend the Spanish government, our Young Pathfinder branch collected to send a grain ship to help the Republicans, and then Harry went off to fight. He was wounded at Aragon, so he was quite a hero to us. But I don't know if I would have married him. We didn't break up exactly. I went off to Teachers' Training College, but we still all met up – it was the War by then – and Rex just walked into the branch one evening – he was on leave. We both knew as soon as we met – this was It.

'There was no animosity involved. We all had discussions about what the government should do, and sat in the dark listening to the wireless – Myra Hess playing Bach, and the Warsaw Concerto. That seemed to hold all our hopes for Poland. Harry was there too, when he was on leave, and he took up with Sheila, and . . . that's how it was.'

'Are those the people who send you a Christmas card?' asked Jandy. A card came every year and was put high on the mantel, with the favourites – 'Season's Greetings to all at Moon Farm, from Harry and Sheila and Mary and Sarah'.

'That's right. We were comrades really, not lovers,' decided Hazel, putting the snap back in the tin. 'We never knew when any of us parted whether we would meet again, whether we'd still be alive. The world was quite different then.'

'What do you think of this one?' – Hazel handed Jandy an old photo, obviously of a young Hazel and Rex in a garden, bent over a toddler. Someone had photographed them when they weren't looking, from an upstairs window perhaps, and then taped over the picture with passe-partout, up and down, so it resembled the view from the bars of a prison.

'How strange. Is that Lynnet as a baby?'

'Yes. It was taken by Liesl – she was staying with us. She stayed for six months, she was a Jewish girl who got in touch when she read a copy of Rex's poetry mag. She was a poet – see – she has written a little poem on the back of the photo.'

Hazel lightly flipped the photo over. 'We both liked her so much. But it became difficult . . . that was the first affair in my marriage, and I found it hard to accept. She left in the end, and sent me this photo, with the poem and letter asking for my forgiveness. I do still hear from her. Not very often.'

' "In a prison/Cut off from the flame of life/I see your joy, I reach out, but it defeats me/condemned always to remain/in my cell." ' Jandy read out, from the back of the snap.

'A strange thing – she'd been in a camp in Germany, and her hands – there were no lines on the palms at all. Completely obliterated. So uncanny. As though her past didn't exist.'

'Have you a photo of her?' demanded Jandy.

'Yes, somewhere. Here we are.' The snap showed a tall, thin, delicate girl, with clouds of dark hair and large features, holding herself hunched and slightly back from life.

'What happened to her?'

'Oh she married quite a long time afterwards, and she wrote to me when she had her little boy. So she's all right. But it took a long time – about fifteen years.'

'Gosh!'

'I should have realised – I thought it was a temporary hitch in the marriage. But it was the first affair of many – heavens, what's the time? – here are the children back. Let's take these pots in and wash them, and then we'll have to get the tea on.'

*   *   *   *

25

b

At the Angel Rex left his companion sleeping soundly and went down to the bar for a quick drink, and to make a telephone call. 'Hello – I'm sorry – are you okay? I couldn't make it to the station, I got caught up in family stuff, it's a bore, but. . .'

'Rex you bastard.'

'Look – I'll be there as soon as I can. Have you everything you need?'

She put the telephone down.

He had another drink, and then trod the deep-carpeted stairs up to the hotel bedroom. She was still sleeping under the four-poster, the sleep of youth, of unconcern. He fetched out his cigarettes again and sat near the window, looking out onto the slope of Angel Hill, dark now but delineated in the light from the hotel. He and Hazel hadn't been close for the past year or so, not really since 1965, when she had refused his suggestion of a communal house, but when he visited had proved amenable in other ways and suddenly piquantly passionate. They hadn't met now for nearly a year. He wondered how he would find her. Visiting Moon Farm was an ordeal for him, he felt attracted and irritated by her and by the world she inhabited and created without him. Moon Farm. He recalled one time, when he had arrived in the middle of a picnic in the garden, Hazel surrounded by her children and their friends. The boys were playing cricket, Shane with his cousin Philip and the Perkyn boy, absorbed in their game. Hebe and Jandy were fidgeting over a doll, small Nick and Jo Perkyn standing nearby and laughing at something, Lynnet and her schoolfriend Alison arguing with Hazel. He had made a remark – he couldn't even remember what it was – something idiotic no doubt and good-natured and silly, that would have been perfectly acceptable anywhere else. They all stopped and looked back at him, Hazel and her brood of young minervas. He had dried up mid-sentence, as though all those grey considering eyes were on the same beast, staring in unison at the interloper, the adult male.

*   *   *   *

Hazel was up at sunrise, to wrap a last minute present and sort the best cutlery. Throwing open the curtains in the sitting room she beheld the garden, and the summer mist floating over the young corn beyond the hedge. It would be a fine day. Across the lawn the golden rod stood in the pale light, a circle of gold in the mist.

She had brought it from Withy House when she left. Alan had loaded the small stuff into his farm van, then called to stop by a very pregnant Hazel.

'I forgot. The golden rod – I wanted to take some roots of it – would you mind?'

'No of course not, my dear.' He had a soft spot for female vulnerability. He backed up near the house, Hazel with difficulty dismounted and rustled through the open bags to find the trowel. She dropped to her knees, digging forcefully between the stiff stems, as yet unflowering.

She and Rex had come to Norfolk from Manchester, to Withy House, with its low ceilings and chunky black beams and back and front stairs, thick walls and small windows, set in an acre of wild ground. Among the grass and trees and primaeval land the golden rod was the sole flower. They were both teaching, Rex part-time whilst he worked on his first book. It was 1950, Rex had started up a poetry magazine, Review Fifty. Poets sent in work from all over the country and the USA. "Literature is a battlefield. . ." began Rex's first editorial. Then Hazel seemed to be pregnant time after time; the heavy East Anglian air, the stillness, the absence of other human beings – seemed to speed up fertility.

As she stood looking out onto Moon Farm garden and the golden rod Hazel felt the subject of the lost baby loom and fade again, a sudden pain, here and then gone.

Alan Barber had turned up on their doorstep one evening, he had seen their address in a copy of Review Fifty, and he announced his interest in poetry. They adopted him straightaway, and spent a giddy summer the three of them, cooking up plans and driving into town, and Rex advised Alan on his love affairs.

'You must write to her father and ask for her hand in

marriage,' Rex advised sagely, when told of Alan's latest love.

'I say, do you really think I should do that?' stumbled Alan.

'Certainly. It is the only socially correct thing to do,' replied Rex with a straight face. 'Come along – we'll compose a letter together – the sooner the better,' he said, and the two of them sat all afternoon, Hazel coming in periodically with refreshments, barely able to contain her laughter at the silliness.

Another time the pair of them had arrived home after an evening at the cinema, to find Alan, who had babysat with Ilse, a visiting friend of theirs, engaged after an evening together. Her husband seemed to object, so that came to nothing.

Then Alan was gored by one of his bulls and he had to spend six months in hospital. He fell in love with several nurses, but there was no Rex to advise him. Then there was the Sister, with her careful makeup and black seamed stockings. This was Margaret, and they had met, become engaged and married within six months, and he brought her back to the farm.

'The poor thing was gored by a bull and then snapped up by the Sister,' Jandy said to Lynnet.

In the room under the eaves of the Angel Rex Marlowe reached for his cigarettes and wondered how he ought to feel, whether he felt enough; whether the feelings were the right ones. As a father many times over he felt swamped with responsibilities and demands – spoken and otherwise – on his emotions. His eldest child had taken the brunt of the divorce, she had been twelve and very resentful.

He recalled Hazel and himself, on the train to their honeymoon. She was a fine girl, she could fight her corner, and she had enthusiasms that were total. When their train had reached Nottingham she was adamant he must meet her college room-mate, who would be getting on to travel home to her parents. She enthusiastically introduced them. Wasn't she the loveliest girl he had ever seen? Look at her dark curly hair, her rosey cheeks, her clear and forceful manner. Rex had agreed – she was the loveliest girl he had ever seen. In the chuntering railway carriage the three of them spoke of the new world, now the war was ended, of the new reforming government, and of their hopes. By the time she left the train they had decided – their first daughter must be called Lynnet, after the Welsh girl who shared their honeymoon carriage. And so it was, baby Lynnet appeared a year later.

He remembered the day she was born. It was the winter of '46-47, temperatures icy. He and Harry Blumenthal, Hazel's old boyfriend, were expectant fathers together. They had gone to the Miller's Arms for a drink, and then walked the Manchester streets, jovially recalling their recent service days and giving one another encouragement. Once at the hospital Rex baulked, and they retreated to the streets again. Harry offered to come and sit in the hospital corridor with him – Sheila was at home, not due for another couple of months. So the pair of them made their way to the maternity ward, through hushed and echoing corridors, air sodden with disinfectant. They sat themselves down on chairs in a cool corridor. Groans came from the ward, and starched nurses bustled about their business.

A fierce little Sister came out and regarded them with suspicion-hostility, he felt.

'Mrs Marlowe has gone into labour,' she announced. 'Which one of you gentlemen is Mr Marlowe?'

Rex indicated himself with a hand at his chest. He almost raised it, as though back as a schoolboy. 'How long will it last?' he asked then.

She shrugged. 'Perhaps a few hours, or it could last a day. You'll have to be patient.'

Off she went, and he was glad she had left, she made him feel guilty. He was responsible for the groans that came from the ward. Harry patted him on the back. 'Cheer up. You've been in tighter holes than this,' he said and Rex silently thought of wartime narrow escapes.

The groans he could hear in the hospital corridor were different from men's groans in the war, they were like animal calls of triumph. Harry patted his top pocket and said, 'I've two cigars waiting.' Bent right forward, his body over his knees, he nodded back.

After what seemed like hours and hours of imprisonment in the antiseptic corridor a nurse brought him a baby wrapped in a cloth. 'A little girl,' she said, smiling.

He peered between the white hallowed cloth and saw a raw face, fold upon fold of red flesh, eyes closed. 'I want to see my wife,' he demanded. The nurse demurred, he insisted, and she fetched the Sister, stiff with pleated fancy bonnet and authority. He was helpless and furious in the face of her power, and in after years Hazel never went into hospital, Rex delivered their babies at home.

'Congratulations. Come along,' said Harry, to make him feel better, 'we must celebrate.' He handed one of the cigars to Rex and they went off to the Florence Nightingale.

The place was shoving with people and Rex turned suddenly garrulous amid the noise. 'What is happening', he announced ponderously, 'is a new civilisation. We are the last gasps of individualism. The future is mass man. We shall not belong in that world, although we have given birth to it. Yes. Not for us to reason why. My daughter – she will feel at home in it. There will be no individuals. Freedom?' – he asked, becoming aware of Harry on his left emanating disapproval.

'You have to ask yourself what freedom really is,' said Harry, 'and how much freedom really exists for the working man?'

'That's it,' Rex took up the theme. 'My comrade here says we have to seriously address the question of freedom for the proletariat. My daughter,' he was shouting now – 'my daughter won't feel the need to stand out from the mass, she will be part of the mass, there will be no works of art by individuals – only mass literature. . .'

He saw Harry's look of deep disapproval. He had gone too far, he was drunk. Moreover, he had just become a father, so cared not for anybody's opinion. 'There won't be individual love either, only mass love – lust, you might say. It. Will. Be – re-*vol*ting,' he pronounced. He never knew how he got home.

A sharp knock came now at the hotel door and breakfast was

30

brought in on a tray. She awoke, yawned and stretched and met his look with a grin, then sat on the pillow, munching her way through a crusty roll. After sudden savage prolonged and sticky kisses he turned and finished his coffee, then hurriedly brushed the shoulders of his suit and smoothed them down.

'How do I look? Do I look sober and God-fearing, as befits the bride's father?' She grinned. He put large hands at her shoulders and looked down at her with the air of ownership that a night's trespass had given him. Then he took a last swipe at his suit with the brush. 'I'll see you anon,' he said from the doorway. Stepping into the corridor humming, he left her licking marmalade off the sheet.

At Moon Farm all were packing into a taxi and Lynnet, leggy in broderie anglaise mini-dress, into the Barbers' car. The children were frisky but careful, for Hebe wore a short summer shift in the same material as Lynnet's dress, and carried a posy, and Nick was in his first long trousers. Two false starts, and they were off, with Alan following Mr Petch, the owner of the local taxi and well-known to the young Marlowes all of their lives.

After raving at the departing car for a full minute and a half, Spotty in his pen gave three dismal yowls and then settled to attempting to bite his back. Saturday quiet lay upon the house, its windows sparkled back in the sunshine, flickering with shadows of leaves.

Inside, the empty house lay strewn with the wreckage of departed life. Towels lay abandoned on the bathroom floor. The record-player hadn't been switched off and stood humming to itself. Down the stairs greenish-yellow light from the panes in the landing window quivered upon crumpled wrapping paper. Half-finished cups of tea and two used sherry glasses stood on the table in the sitting room. Smoke hovered above the ash-trays and splinters of fire like worms still moved eating at itself.

In the larder lay the flans for the evening, slices of tomato and mushroom surfacing from the still seas of cheese. Cider stood in a big flagon, with clusters of small lemonade and Babycham bottles for the children. A monster peach trifle, its turrets and flutings under chocolate hail. A big ham in silver foil and trays of eggs stood on the cool slate shelf of the home farm. A crock of homemade pâté, carefully covered. Simple food, cooked by Hazel and Margaret for the family party that evening.

Rex came speeding up the stairs of St. Edfric's Registry Office, going quickly through to where the other guests were gathered. There was no sign of the bride and an awkward hush fell at his entrance. Then Hazel appeared to ask them to wait, Lynnet was suffering from nerves. Rex glared at her hat atop of her round smirking face, and thought she had never looked more pleased with herself. After about ten minutes Lynnet came in and he cheered up – a pretty girl in a summer dress, with her flowers.

Forty people sat at table in the banqueting room of the Angel Hotel. Sunlight streamed in upon glass and flowers, upon the wedding guests laughing and chattering and eating, exchanging reminiscences and anecdotes and having their glasses refilled between courses.

On the table stood big glass bowls of strawberries and cherries in wine. Behind the wedding cake with its mounting tiers sat Lynnet and Jonathan, looking away from one another towards the guests, every so often turning and sharing a quick look. Rex sat next to Betty, Jonathan's mother, and nodded sagaciously as she told him of the struggle she'd had to get him to eat as a child. He glared over to where Hazel sat under her hat, looking, he thought, colossally smug.

Carefully stage-managed, waiters appeared suddenly, whisking white cloths in one hand and with the other holding high above their heads on fingers making a perfect vee between thumb and forefinger, platters of crinoline ladies. Accompanied by 'aaaahs' of wonder and surprise from the guests they proceeded deftly to scoop ice-cream and sponge out of pink and white frilly skirts.

'It doesn't seem five minutes', Mrs Grove, Hazel's mother, told Margaret, 'since Hazel and Rex were married. Those two – they were so much in love.' Margaret smiled and nodded sympathetically and touched the stone in her engagement ring.

Over at the end of the room the elderly aunts from Manchester captured Hebe and examined her and asked questions about Jonathan. How long had Lynnet known him? What was he reading at Cambridge? Did – with lowered voices – Rex approve?

'How goes it?' Rex came up behind Alan and spoke enthusiastically, as though they had last met a week or so ago. Alan was overjoyed to see his old friend. 'You've ceased to farm, I hear.'

'Yes, I'm at Knope and Partners, insurance brokers. What about you?'

'My next book is out shortly. And I'm working for Shell as an in-house journalist. . .'

Once again Alan succumbed to Rex's charm – no, it wasn't charm, he could have withstood charm. It was a hail-fellow-well-met exuberance, we're-all-in-this-crazy-world-together cheerfulness. When he came and sat near Alan felt again the great pull Rex had on him in the early days. He still fondly recalled a party at the Marlowes in the early fifties. He had brought two old school friends, Michael Turner and Peter Dorrell. There were nurses from the local hospital, and very pregnant Hazel had sat talking sympathetically to a miserable young poet, whilst Rex mixed drinks. 'I say Rex – you weren't really a communist?' Alan had asked, shocked and semi-delighted.

'Not only that,' proclaimed Rex, 'but you are all going to partake of my special anti-capitalist punch,' – and with rolled up shirt-sleeves had maniacally mixed sherry with Tizer and cut lemons. 'Here we are – my own concoction – it's called the Red Peril,' he had said, ladling out glasses of the stuff and handing it about.

'So you work for Shell now then!' Alan responded over the

33

wedding table litter of cake crumbs and spilled wine.

Rex gave a broad grin. 'Yes, I'm taking the dirty dollar,' he said. 'It pays somewhat better and I can't manage on the money I make from writing.'

'You surprise me. I see your books are everywhere.'

'Oh there's no problem with the sales, but I don't make enough. . .'

'Ah well, nobody ever makes enough,' pointed out Alan.

The Barbers hadn't seen Rex for some years, although they heard of his doings frequently from Hazel. After Rex's suggestion of a communal household was turned down by Hazel, the pair of them had become involved again, restarted their affair. Alan shook his head, Margaret looked to heaven, and both had pronounced darkly on the outcome. Hazel and Rex had decided to give a reunion party, inviting all their old friends for an evening together. Alan and Margaret adamantly refused to go.

'Absolutely not,' said Margaret, turning to Madeleine, their French friend. 'Are you going, Madeleine?'

'Nooooooo Margrrrrrrret, not when I think 'ow 'e left 'er. Michael, my Englishman, I can't tell 'im what to do, 'e is going.'

So of all their old friends, only Michael turned up. Faced with social ostracism, Hazel realised they wouldn't be able to go back to the past.

'You have children now?' enquired Rex, making himself agreeable to Margaret.

'Yes, we do. We have a little boy of eight, Jasper, and Victoria is four,' she smiled happily.

'Maternity suits you,' he remarked pleasantly, meaning it.

Over the tables eleven year old Nick and his father regarded each other suspiciously, each aware they were required to speak to the other. From across the room Hazel anxiously watched them exchange a few words. Rex was slightly awkward, uneasy with the boy, felt he had no hold on him. Because Rex had absconded by the time the baby was born Hazel had named it herself and not the name chosen by him. 'Nicholas!' Rex had bellowed down the telephone, 'whatever sort of name is that?'

'Well you weren't here to register the birth and it was good enough for your pseudonym when you were writing pot-boilers,' she batted back.

'Pot-boilers to keep you and your children in food and clothes,' he raged.

'My children *and* your children,' she snapped, and slammed the telephone down on its cradle. When Gillian had her baby a few months later, it was named Thor – the name Rex had chosen for Nick. This was related with much spirit by Hazel to Alan and Margaret and friends, and received by them with indignant relish, as it was meant to be.

'Well goodness me, Hazel,' said Margaret.

Margaret and Mrs Grove sat together talking of their children. Margaret had a soft spot for the old lady, although her opinions were liable to seem alarming. Hazel's mother – Elizabeth Acre, socialist and suffragette. Now the sharp outline of her youthful self was muted into Bessie or Gran, warm and dumpy and still wearing the Edwardian bodies from her youth, with lace windows set into them. But, as she explained to Margaret, she had actually been a suffragist.

'Oh yes. We were with Mrs Despard – you see, not all men had a vote in those days. There was a property qualification. . .' Margaret smiled back, she admired Mrs Grove, for although into her eighties she did voluntary work at the Stopes Clinic, which had been founded in Manchester to help working women avoid pregnancy.

('She thinks if she can stop everybody having children all the world's problems will be solved,' Hazel had said scornfully. 'You must have been a disappointment to her then,' Margaret pointed out, and they both rocked with laughter.)

Mr Grove, Hazel's father, sat back from the table and watched the young people all around. Pushing ninety, he was still not retired. Each morning he went to his workshop, full of wood-shavings and partly-turned pieces of wood, which were to become hat blocks. There wasn't the call for them now, society had changed. The old man remembered the days when the workshop was full and the work kept on coming – when he was a young man at the beginning of the century. He recalled the ladies' hats then, which resembled large platters filled with fruit and flowers, feathers, lace. Policemen's helmets, officers caps, mayors' hats, naval headgear – all heads were measured carefully, the corresponding hat blocks chiselled from wood, and the hats carefully modelled around them. Afterwards the hat blocks were numbered and stored, individual to individual heads, waiting for the next time the owner required a new hat. The hat was an indication of its owner's position in the social hierarchy. Hatless persons were the hoi-polloi, the discounted, the ones without status. Married ladies, men going respectably to their work – all wore hats.

The large old man had seen much change, and took everything in around him with a sunny smile. In his long life he had been to many weddings, but this was the first of his grandchildren to marry, and the first bride he had seen with bare head.

Hazel looked round the room for Rex, but he wasn't there. Then she sought Lynnet among the chattering guests, but the Bride had taken her flowers and slipped from the Angel. Crossing the little eighteenth century square, she entered the Abbey, cold in the sunshine, and lodged the great door behind her. What need was there that she, an atheist, was drawn to come here on her wedding day? She hadn't wanted white or veils or a religious service, yet the Abbey meant something to her that she couldn't understand. As a schoolgirl she had sung here with St. Edfric's Girls' Grammar; she had done a project on the saint in the Fourth Form, and as a Saturday librarian had fixed drawing pins in a display of his life and times. She moved up the side aisle and went to stand under the great Eye of God, held in place by its mediaeval bosses, looking down on her as it had looked down on folk for over seven hundred years.

Motes spun round in the cold and jewelled light, they cast trembling shadows on the Bride. She went to stand in front of an effigy – an Elisabeth Frink sculpture of the boy saint. He looked out toward life with blank unflinching eyes, his limbs at one with his drawn sword, held in front of him like a living cross; bare coronet firmly in place on shorn head. As schoolgirls they had used to joke his mother had made him have a pudding basin haircut. The sword he held straight and downward, not like a prop, like a pattern for the growth of his own spare limbs. Lynnet stared closely at his unseeing eyes. He was ten when he was martyred. She thought of the boy and all that had accrued around him; then reverently laid her flowers and ferns between his spurred stone feet.

In the Angel Rex felt he had come prepared to be on his best behaviour, but that hat was liable to bring out the worst in him. He stifled his feelings in the interest of the general good. At least he could make an escape. Hazel was having her way, this whole business was created by her and paid for by him, and he felt he owed it to himself to sidestep it in some way. He didn't see why he shouldn't do his own thing – that's what they called it now. Leaving the throng to ring his secretary, back to mingle with the guests, and out again and up the hotel stairs to take almost by force a young female – one of the Moon Farm enemy – still sitting stupefied from the last time.

In the hotel room Jandy sat naked and wrapped about in a tapestried coverlet from the bed. Her eyes wandered aimlessly over the room, with its unopened curtains and permanent frozen summer in the carved grapes and flowers on the bed-head. The tapestry drapes were stitched with scampering rabbits and frayed pinks, squirrels and strange little helmeted birds; periwinkle spread delicate tendrils and does were settled among strawberry flowers. It was very still here, as she traced with her eye all the minutiae of a mediaeval garden she could hear nothing of the festivities below.

She was still sitting wrapped in the coverlet, mind wandering, not thinking of anything. Rex appeared in the doorway. He ripped the coverlet from her but didn't stop to take off his own clothes. After he had taken her she blindly helped him straighten his clothes, and he departed. She was left looking at a wisp of confetti in the damp palm of her hand. A pink horseshoe, for luck. Not a heart.

For Rex afterwards the whole wedding vision of them — guests, and food and flowers, broderie anglaise Bride, hatted and chattering relations — was an interlude between bouts of sweet hot lust. He talked easily and smiled and nodded and drank, and then went upstairs again.

The next time he came she was waiting for him, hot and ecstatic, she flew across the room at him, couldn't wait for him to put his fingers all over her again and bring her alive.

'Bring me some wedding cake,' she had demanded. Rex produced some from his pocket. 'How is it you aren't partaking of it downstairs?' he enquired, watching her wolfing it.

She shrugged. 'Wasn't asked.' This was the norm. She was never taken to family weddings as a child. Her existence was felt to be an embarrassment to Margaret.

'You're supposed to put it under your pillow and make a wish. Not devour it straightaway.'

'I'm starving,' she pointed out, handling the wedge of sticky cake, with its cement of icing and marzipan.

Off he went again. Alone in the hotel bedroom once more, she looked down at the plump palms of her hands and thought of the hands of Liesl, empty of lines.

They all posed for a last photograph on the steps of the Angel, with its white columns and bright green creeper encrusting the front. Then Lynnet and Jonathan climbed into a shiny black car adorned with white satin bows, and drove to the station, which they could have walked to quite easily, but everything was different today. The guests lined up to wave, watching the car as it turned heavily in the small space of Angel Hill. Then, shaking hands and kissing they either took their leave of one another or collected together to go home. Some of the relations were driving back to Manchester, Mr and Mrs Grove and Hazel's sister Helen were going back with the Marlowes.

'Oh do let's go back the Farthingale way,' said Hebe. She loved to see Moon Farm across the fields, coming towards them out of the corn.

2

HOTEL

'Come along, foundling,' said Rex heartily, breezing into the hotel bedroom. 'We're going to eat and then have a walk round.'

'Can't we go somewhere else?'

'We can go somewhere else if that's what you'd prefer, but I must eat soon. A proper meal of good red meat, not wedding cake. Get yourself ready and we'll be off.'

'I am ready, nearly. Are you going to Moon Farm while you're round here?' she called over her shoulder, on the way into the bathroom. He shook his head. He hadn't been asked to the family party.

He felt like a stranger there, an intruder. He entered *her* home, intimidated and wondering, shot through with a kind of fractiousness, yet thrilled that his woman was such a real person. She could manage without him. Sometimes this infuriated him. At other times they both realised it was untrue.

As Jandy pottered about and brushed her hair he smoked and thought to one time. After a row with Gillian he had driven furiously away through the night, all the way to Moon Farm, arriving early in the dark morning and sleeping in the car, which he parked at the end of the deserted lane. Waking in the first light he watched the mist swirl over the corn and the sun rise, drizzle fall from the hedgerows, and then he crept about the outside of the house in the unearthly stillness of the garden.

Golden rod, stiff and unremarkable in the dawn light; from the buddleia he realised a cat watched him and he found its gaze disconcerting. He watched the unblinking windows – they would be packed inside sleeping, eyelids drawn down – his woman, his children. There was a stillness here that couldn't be broken, he stole about the lawn as the day dawned, until from the house side floated the high-pitched sound of children's voices. Then, frightened to break the spell, for he knew he couldn't enter this enchanted world, it existed without him, he ran for his car and drove off into the day before he was seen.

'There, I'm ready,' said Jandy. He clapped his hands to her shoulders approvingly.

After they had eaten in the hotel dining room he insisted they have a stroll. As they passed the desk on the way out the receptionist called 'Mr Marlowe? – will you and Mrs Marlowe be having lunch tomorrow? Would you like to order it now?' Jandy laughed and walked on, leaving Rex to sort it out.

'I hate being called Mrs – it's a form of address denoting subservience,' she said when he rejoined her.

Rex, who thought females should be subservient, scowled and said, 'What about you – aren't you going to marry?'

'Marriage is stupid,' she decreed.

'It's a way of ensuring the young are cared for,' he replied severely.

She stuck her tongue out at him.

They strolled about the small town. In the mood to chat now that sex and food instincts had been sated, he asked her questions about her life, and what she was doing in St. Edfric's.

'I've just come from a conference at Kessingland, on World Revolution,' she said, simple and grand. Her head was spinning with arguments and images – a bearded marxist Jesuit priest talking French and playing football on the beach; the loos with battered splintery doors swaying in the wind, 'Leaders Only' printed on the end one – obviously used by ancient brownie packs; a discussion on 'How should society be run?' led by a Cambridge professor and a factory worker. Everybody gathering in the Games Room, which was an old war-time hangar, Dionne Warwick on the nickelodeon. Every day breakfast of tinned spaghetti and fishcakes. 'Somebody's idea of a joke?' people asked.

'No it was cheap, and you can organise it next time,' answered Andrew, the Camp Organiser belligerently.

'And I jolly well hope we're not having spaghetti and fishcakes for breakfast tomorrow,' she finished up.

They walked across Angel Hill and along Hatter Street to the abbey.

'Ah, the hatters of this world,' began Rex, in his slight Cheshire rasp. 'It's remarkable, but the power of the hatter to socially divide people and put them in their place is on the wane. You may think that's progress – yet how many new things are springing up to do that very thing. . .'

'You know Rex I don't know why you aren't still a communist, you sound like one sometimes.'

'Being a communist requires a degree of bright-eyed innocence of which I am no longer capable.'

Crossing the road they made for the abbey gardens and the magnificent abbey gate. 'This was some place in the Middle Ages,' said Rex. 'The land here was dominated by the abbey and the abbot of St. Edfric's was a big noise in the land. There was a stroppy population here too,' he added enthusiastically. 'The townsfolk were always revolting. Probably because they were relatively well-off.'

'That's where Alan works,' – Jandy pointed to a small eighteenth-century square facing them.

'We've known Alan a long time. Ever since we came to Withy House.'

'Yeh I know. And there was a party there and you made a punch called the Red Peril. He's told me.'

Rex was terribly touched. 'Did he remember that?'

Over towards the sunset lay the abbot's bridge, carrying a footpath and acting as the perimeter of the abbey across the river. Each of its arcs had a portcullis, which could be lowered to prevent entry into the abbey grounds by boat. The bridge was strengthened by flying buttresses and gabled piers, and surrounded by trees whose soft leaves seemed to float in the summer breeze. They paused, silent, the hush engulfed them.

Then they moved towards the massive gate, rebuilt at the abbot's direction when the first one was burnt down by the local populace after the Black Death. Short of money and labour, the abbey put an instant toll on travellers passing through, a tithe on all tenants of the abbey lands and folk who grazed their animals, and they sought to borrow money from the local Jews, those who hadn't been slaughtered in the outbreak of violence. They gave freely, and between lattices of praying Norman warriors and coroneted princes, two great stars of David were splayed into the final perpendicular gate, as a thank you for help to the Cistercian foundation.

St. Edfric's and the other wool towns were prosperous and rising in the Middle Ages. Rex and Jandy looked up the narrow lane, the site of a pogrom. Afterwards, the only Jewish family left had built a fine stout house, the ground floor a prison – thick stone walls and no windows – the upstairs light and airy, hung with rich tapestries and carpets and every kind of luxury.

'Come along – I'll show you another strange house,' – and he took off through a cobbled sidestreet by the abbey, Jandy following, until they came to a tall narrow building.

'This was the house of Leofric the One-Eyed. He had been a crusader, imprisoned, converted to Islam and eventually released by the Saracens. When he returned he brought with him a Saracen. The local populace rioted and burned the abbey, pursued the Jews and slew them, yet Leofric strode among them alone, disliked and greatly feared, yet none dare raise a hand to him or to the Saracen.'

They wandered through the Abbey gardens and into the rose garden, a gift from an American stationed at St. Edfric's during the War. It was a perfect square where only red roses bloomed, tiny and brilliant; four paths led to a sundial. They stood at the heart of perfection surveying its form, and a duck waddled in on strong leathery feet, destroying the smoothness with its dry comedian quacking, whacking each leathery foot down on the path and going noisily into bushes. Jandy laughed and thought of telling Hazel, as one does think of people you like with whom to share a joke.

42

Once in the Abbey they stood under the great eye of God which had looked down on generations for over seven hundred years. The boy St. Edfric – someone had laid summer flowers at his feet. 'He reminds me of Dale Perkyn,' said Jandy.

All around the stations of the Cross glinted colours into the gloom, and in the rose window at the rear were fixed a leafy Adam and Eve. 'A bit of stained glass cheek from the local populace, no doubt,' said Rex with gusto. ' "When Adam delved and Eve span/Who was then the gentleman?" ' He let out a hoot of laughter. 'Those old abbots must have been quite some diplomats, in their way,' he said then, turning to survey the great Star of David window.

'As I told you, Leofric the One-Eyed and the Saracen struck terror into the townsfolk, but he went about his business unmolested, and look here, I'll show you something.' He went to a side of the abbey and instructed Jandy to place her feet in a certain position. 'Now what can you see? Look there – there – over on that pillar.' She peered around a pillar and saw where light was thrown in through a clear upper window from a window outside, which cast a shadow on the opposite pillar.

'Is it – I can see. . . a crescent moon – is that what you mean?'

His laughter echoed about the slabbed stone. 'That's exactly what I mean. Leofric built his tall house so that the shape of the crescent window hit inside the abbey, and yet nothing has been violated, there are no artefacts within the walls.'

'You've lost me,' said Jandy, 'and I'm tired.'

He looked her over and said, 'I take it that's a veiled hint that you want to go back to bed.'

Later, back at the hotel bedroom, when they put the light back on, she said critically, 'There's too much sex in your books.'

He looked back at her with amazement, kept his temper, and said carefully, 'Sex is part of human activity – as you seem to know. After all, I'm just a twentieth century Christian savage. And it's only 550,000 years since Man differentiated himself from the other primates. So what do you suggest I write about?'

'Well, sci-fi is a way of avoiding the class struggle. You should really be writing something to take the working class forward.'

Robustly and with a reasonable air, Rex pointed out, 'But I don't want to take the working class forward. In fact, I can say quite categorically – I do not care about the working class.'

'I thought you'd been a communist,' – her tone implied she wouldn't be here had she known otherwise.

'I'm not a communist now. For one thing, I'd like to be king.'

'Oh really? How very difficult for you.'

'Difficult? No it isn't difficult. I don't expect the world to be made in the image of my desires. I expect my own efforts to win whatever advantage I have.'

She was silent. These ideas confused her, she couldn't square them with the fact of his physical authority.

'But what about a society of equals?' she finally offered.

Rex wasn't interested. 'I don't believe in equals. It's an abstraction. It's not even a pretty myth.'

'So what is the best form of government, then?' she asked bleakly, sitting on the pillow and kicking at the bedclothes.

'The best governments there have ever been – in reality, not on paper – have been benevolent dictatorships. Everything works together in those circumstances – it has to! – and the benevolent dictator has the power of mercy.'

'And just how do you ensure the dictator is going to be benevolent?'

He grinned and took a drink from the tumbler on the bedside table. 'That's the problem. You can't.'

She looked scornfully back at him. 'You don't care about the working class, you don't like the unions. . .'

'The despotism of the weak,' jeered Rex.

'Well if you're so keen on dictators, presumably you don't mind despotism.'

'Oh don't give me that. The dictator is a single man. The unions are mass man. And I don't like mass man. The unions are still fighting wars that were essentially over years ago – they object to a moneyed elite. The only meaningful elite are the scientists. They are going to lift Mankind from this planet.'

On this upbeat note they abandoned the argument, Rex splashed cold water on his face and left the hotel for a late night stroll.

Left to her own devices Jandy fetched out the chocolate and recalled the first times she had met Rex and Hazel. When she visited the newly married pair Alan had driven them to Withy House one evening. Rex fixed them all drinks – Lynnet aged eleven and Jandy at thirteen had lemonade-shandy – and then he had stood before them all and held forth on his views on the way the world was going.

'And what Rex,' Alan had asked, sure of something delightfully awful coming, 'is your opinion of the Bible?'

'The Bible – collection of entertaining stories, no more factually true than the Arabian Nights. And I speak as one who is obliged to teach Scripture.'

Afterwards, as they drove home in the Suffolk darkness, tree branches coming alight in the car headlights and disappearing into the night again, Alan said to Margaret, 'Rex – he's very amusing company of course, I couldn't possibly hope to match him in conversation. But darling, I do hope you don't take too much notice of what he says.'

'Oh darling – as though I would,' answered Margaret, who sometimes didn't take all that much notice of what he said either. In the backseat, schoolgirl Jandy said nothing, but saved this up to tell the parents at home. The Barbers' habit of calling each other darling all the time was an endless source of amusement to Margaret's parents. 'Now darling,' her mother would say to her father, 'would you like me to cut you some sand-witches?'

'Oh no darling, we mustn't have sand-witches now, it will spoil our luncheon.'

'Now darling, don't forget your napkin ring. . .' the old couple tee-heed at one another over their daughter's airs and graces.

Jandy was shining-eyed over the evening. Hazel and Rex were the most glamorous people she had ever met. Hazel arched her brows and cracked back smart rejoinders at her man, like the fast-talking ladies in the old films, the Myrnas and Caroles and Gingers. Rex had written a book and drove a cadillac and said the word bastard a lot.

To Margaret and Alan and Hazel and Rex the Future seemed but an interesting possibility – that possibility that is akin to impossibility. They made jokes about it and furnished a scenario for it, based on Rex's scientific readings.

'None of us will cook, mealtimes will be pills,' they assured one another, laughing as Rex replenished the Woolworths' tumblers with red wine, Lynnet and Jandy fat as ticks on fizzy lemonade, three year old Shane upstairs having his nap, Hazel's new washing-machine – a wonder to them all – doing all of their washing. When they went in the afternoons they often watched a film together – the films of their youth. The curtains at Withy House didn't need to be closed to shade the television screen, for the windows were set deeply into thick walls.

Rex kept up with the world of science as well as literature and current affairs, and always had an opinion on whatever cropped up. He gave people the assurance that he knew what he was talking about, his opinions were definite ones and he provided confidence for others. 'As I stand here,' he had declaimed before the brick fireplace, empty on the summer evening, 'I know I will pass away but I firmly predict. . .'

Try as she might Jandy couldn't remember what he had predicted, she only remembered his confidence, insouciance, his asserting himself before them all and making a stand.

The summer she left school she went to stay in East Anglia for the long holiday, staying first with Margaret and Alan, then with Rex and Hazel. She had slept in the oldest part of Withy House, a small hardly used sitting room. Excited, she couldn't sleep, the cold in that part of the house was intense. She kept the light on all night, read some of the books, passing from one to another, restless. That evening each child had been sent to bed in order of age – Shane first, then Lynnet. Older than Lynnet and also a guest, she had been allowed to stay up with Hazel and Rex and watch a grown-up play on the television. When it finished she said 'Goodnight' politely, and never forgot how she left them. Rex had his left arm across the back of the sofa, behind Hazel, a beer in his right hand. They looked like lovers spending an intimate evening together, not like married people. Afterwards, she always wondered if they had conceived Nick that evening.

The next day Hazel had said, 'How would you like a job called Looking After Baby? In the country – lovely family – plenty of free time – as many books to read as you want. . .' And she had put her hand lightly round Jandy's shoulder and looked at Rex.

Staying here was everything she most wanted, and unbelievingly she heard her own voice say, 'I'd love to, but I have a job waiting for me.' She never understood why she lied.

That final summer Rex had lent her a book with a fantastical Queen on the cover, sandy-haired and ruffed, black and gold and tawny, with great wings of stiff net, like a full-bodied gorgeous butterfly. Jandy read it and brought it back the following summer, but he had gone.

She turned back into the room from the window, seeing Rex, now back, on the bed smoking and reading a science journal. She wondered where he had been, and suddenly remembered her gran's opinion of him, although they had never met – 'Some men want their tails cutting off.' She smiled involuntarily.

'Why the merriment, wench?' His Elizabethanisms were conscious and dedicated acts of homage.

'Oh nothing. I was just thinking about my grandmother – she brought me up.'

'Your grandmother, the Barbers, Hazel – I see you have a multiplicity of parents,' remarked Rex.

'Yeh well. What about you – you have a multiplicity of females, wives and suchlike.' She meant mistresses, but it seemed a rather grand word.

'Oh, young people now,' he shrugged. 'Like yourself – living with a man, sleeping with another, in love with a third. Do you really like living in that way?' he asked unbelievingly.

'What other way could I live, if I'm honest?' she asked.

He shook his head. 'When we were young we wanted to be with each other and to make a life together,' he called at her back, as she went through to the hotel bathroom to wash a top. 'We didn't want just the passing moment.'

'Maybe that's because that's all you might have had. We have a whole lifetime ahead of us. . . ' she called back.

'Yes, things were different then, we had just fought a war,' he mused, as she returned.

'Yes I know. And your love affair was something special, that not many people have.'

He was brought up sharp, taken aback. 'What do you know about our love affair?'

She paused before answering. 'It's my favourite fairytale,' she said, laying her head against his arm.

From the hotel bedroom she watched rain splash down onto roofs and into guttering, and thought of the sodden fields beyond the town and of Farthingale, where the electricity would probably be off now.

With a sigh she turned back into the room and demanded 'Tell me some more about Leofric.'

Rex stretched from the bed and poured himself another drink, filling the glass nearly to the brim, and then he held out his other arm for her to go to him. 'Listen, my infant, and you will become wise in the ways of men. Leofric as I have told you, lusted after the knowledge which lay beyond his world. As a young man he had read heathens, and knew of the strange monetary system in Cathay – it was all pieces of paper. He read that the world was round, that you couldn't fall off the edge – which is what everyone around him in St. Edfric's thought. He knew of Roger Bacon, who foretold machines would one day fly through the air, and of Isidore of Seville, who spoke of atoms. The Church taught that the Plague was caused by humours and the influence of the planets, but a Moor in Salerno wrote that it was caused by infection.

'So he found himself on the road to Jerusalem, and then

captured by the Saracens. He got on well with them, they shared much of their knowledge and their astronomy with him, and he welcomed new experiences, and observing the stars in the Moor's glass he knew he had been freed from the limitations of western christianity. So after Leofric's return to the town he and the Saracen settled themselves down in the long tall house off Hatter Street, and in the course of time both took to themselves lusty local talent. Leofric dallied with Margarita, who for some reason that escapes me for the minute was a royal ward. . .'

'You've pinched that out of the Black Arrow.'

'Nonsense. And Ibn – Leo called him Ibby – took up with one Bridget Tapster, who ran her own tavern and didn't give a button for local gossip. Of course, they could have several wives – Islam has a realistic idea of an adult male's sexuality,' averred Rex.

'You would think of that.'

'Let's get something straight. If I'm to tell this story I require silence on your part. Is that understood?'

'Oh okay.'

'And Margarita wore a hennin and Bridget – who was really most comely – a wimple that quite set off her pretty little dimple. If you insist on putting your hand there I shall not be able to continue with the story – thank you. Leofric of course dabbled in the Black Arts, when he wasn't with Margarita he stayed up at nights among his rows of bubbling tubes and his black cat, and regularly when the moon was full he sought the Philosopher's Stone. He wasn't so bothered about changing base metal into gold – he didn't have the gold fetish so prevalent now – but he knew that's what alchemists hankered after so did it now and then to keep his hand in. He could raise a tempest, and he conjured for Margarita a ravishing gown in a lost colour – delicia – a sumptuous mix of gold and pink that is beyond our imaginings because beyond our sense experience – a tint we no longer have the ability to apprehend.

'Leofric had a tame raven – Kronk – not a rare bird then, for in the preceding centuries the fields of East Anglia had been littered with ravens feasting on the bodies of Angles slaughtered by the heathen Danes. And Kronk and his master

49

had an understanding, they had been together for a long time.

'Now Ibby was getting a touch homesick, he had a lady called Layla back home, but he knew Bridget, although but a tavern keeper, was a princess among women. Leofric, as an alchemist, could do all kinds of things we can't do now. He could – for a short time only – see through to different times, and communicate with people from other ages. He didn't do it often because it gave him a bad headache. Back home Layla was getting restive, so Leo and Ibby decided to make one last trip. Now in those days "going on a trip to Jerusalem" was the expression for getting blind drunk on the mead they imbibed then. Strong stuff. And they had forgotten it was also the name of the drinking establishment run by Bridget. So when they uttered their imprecation "O unseen forces, take us on the Trip to Jerusalem" they landed – thump – on their bottoms in the tap room just as Bridget was changing the barrels. She scolded them well and boxed both their ears. As you can imagine, they were somewhat discouraged by these turn of events. But later that evening, they repaired to Leofric's lunary, which housed all his lenses for viewing the heavens, and was in the opposite end of the house from the solar, which they inhabited by day. And by concentrating very hard Leofric managed to reach Layla through the ether, so that Ibby and she could speak. She was very well, she said, and looking forward to seeing them soon. She also spoke of a document she had put in Ibby's satchel – surely he had found it by now? – she had specially wrapped it together with the spiced lamb pasties and the koftes and pomegranate fruit, because perusal of it would show how their fortune could be made. Had he not found it? Ibby hummed and haaa-ed a little – the truth was, he had eaten the food and discounted the parchment and wiped his greasy fingers on the delicate lace kerchiefs, so lovingly worked by Layla. Layla said she had a wonderful bulb, she kept it for his return, knowing it would make their fortune. It was already now putting out roots – couldn't he hurry. Ibby shook his head madly and gesticulated to Leofric to cut the connexion. Layla's bright face faded, and they were left looking at the pots and tubes and Kronk regarding them from the top of a telescope with a sarcastic eye.

'Leo and Ibby rummaged through the leather satchels they had brought with them, and finally found the parchment among a litter of old pasty crumbs. Kronk started kronking triumphantly and Leofric had to shush him by batting him off the telescope.

'Breaking open the seal, Leofric scanned the old writing – it was written in Babylonian – as quickly as he could, it told of a bulb, which would flower into a rose – a marvellous rose, unlike any other. And the story of this flower was also written down in the parchment. Leofric read of Solomon's head gardener, who lived in his own world of seedlings and cuttings and graftings, he experimented with colour and form, and he managed to cultivate a rose with a message in writing and a picture on its petals of the glorious Sabaea – that's Sheba to you and me.

'Now when he heard this Solomon was angry but he knew it ill became a great ruler to allow a base thing such as jealousy to dictate his actions, which must be measured and merciful at all times. And after all, he did have a thousand wives of his very own. But strangely – that made no difference to his pique. The wives anyway were little more than a liability, he couldn't remember all their birthdays and he was fed up with their babies and their inter-wife scrapping.

'So then Solomon summoned the head gardener – whose name was Ali – and said to him, "I see that not content with having control over my most imperial gardens and the imperial fountains and all the courts of Shemel-Nessin and the fig trees of Phul-nana" – did I hear you giggle?'

'No. Not at all.'

'Good. "Not content", enunciated Solomon the All-Wise, "with having great control over my most imperial gardens and all therein, you have taken to portraiture on the quiet."

'Ali bowed low and replied: "O most high and dread sovereign, whatever I do I do to your glory" – and he didn't lift so much as an eyelash but kept his eyes on the floor, where the carpet dazzled him with all the colours of Babylon.

' "Hmmmmph," harrumphed Solomon, thinking hard.

51

'Head gardeners were hard to come by – and so for that matter were kitchen scullions – ones that were any good. On the other hand, the gardener had forgotten himself and Solomon knew only too well the result of letting things get out of hand. . .'

'What about asking Sheba whether she minded?'

'That wouldn't do any good. She was his favourite wife and the moon of his desire because she wanted what he wanted,' Rex replied smugly. 'Lèse-majesté might sound like a joke to such bird-brains as yourself and the Moon Farm contingent, but the ramifications can be far more serious than they sound.'

'Well you've got him into a right pickle now.'

'Yes. That's life. So Solomon thought for a while and then asked his head gardener, "You must have studied them well – can you tell me the exact tint of the Empress's eyes?"

'All sorts of colours ran through the gardener's mind, but he was too perspicacious to utter them. He said only, "O most wise and bountiful lord, I am afraid I was too busy to notice." He was dismissed with a wave of the royal hand. Temporarily assuaged, Solomon let the subject drop. And yet he was not satisfied. The idea that Sheba's face might soon be blooming in gardens all over the land did not at all please him and – reluctantly – he issued orders for all the bulbs in the garden to be seized. When he heard this the head gardener's heart broke, he took the bulb and absconded. He was brought back a few day's later, searched, and thrown into prison. The bulb could not be found.

'After a while Solomon relented. Of course, it was the Ancient World so they didn't have habeas corpus, but even so there was a rudimentary sense of justice and Solomon, wisest of the wise, knew it was unjust to imprison a man indefinitely on a whim. Such behaviour compromises authority, which must be seen to have some degree of fairness. The gardener was let out and allowed back to his old job. He planted tasteful beds of alyssum and lobelia – quite nice really, but not a patch on the splendour of the former gardens, with their cool scented fountains, their banks of pink lilies, camphor plants and humming birds, orange groves and luscious flowering fig trees.

'Solomon took it meekly, he knew if you break a man's spirit you can expect tidy flowerbeds and nasty little notices saying Keep off the Grass. It was peeving too because nobody dared suggest planting roses, which they needed to make attar of roses, and in the harem the odalisques were livid, they muttered to each other, "How can we be proper odalisques without attar of roses – it's absurd" – they pouted and sulked – as little people often will do – but they dared not voice their opinion openly. So when Solomon, worn by cares, called for some carnal relaxation they took it out on him in small ways – and a harem full of recalcitrant odalisques is no joke. Only Sheba was sympathetic, she stroked his brow and made him soothing tisanes. Solomon went to see the gardener in his shed, he sat with him on an old packing case and spoke with him man to man.

' "I didn't know what to do," confessed Solomon, the Mighty, the Wisdom of the World. "You see," he said humbly, looking up from his dusty seat on the packing case, "I'm in charge of the known world and I have a heavy responsibility. . ." And the gardener nodded and puffed on his pipe and said nothing. And eventually he agreed to manage the gardens himself personally, to attend to the pink lilies and maybe look out some rose seedlings. But the bulb that had caused all the trouble was never found.

'Now when he had finished reading the parchment Leofric knew that here was a Quest, and it would cost much gold and time, but he knew anyway you had to lose Everything in order to gain in the metaphysical sense – which, being Leofric, was the sense that mattered to him.

'So he sold his possessions to pay for the journey, and shut up the house off Hatter Street. The pair of them and the raven took their farewells of Margarita and Bridget, and set out once more for Jerusalem, to find Layla and the precious bulb. They crossed at Harwich and made their way down through the provinces of France, and then Spain. And they had a good time when they got to Spain, for the Moors were in control again just then, and they were greeted as long-lost brothers in Islam, by people they didn't know. Kronk quite took to all the feasting and being made much of, and as it was to turn very hot when they got to Palestine, Leofric decided to leave him at the home of a generous Moorish captain, who promised to look after him until they returned.

'Layla was overjoyed to see them when they turned up on the doorstep, she cooked their favourite meal and then took them to the rooftop, where she kept the bulb. Well it was just coming into flower, and all Palestine held its breath as the rose began to slowly open its petals.

'And it flowered and they saw the message written on the rose and the face of Sheba, and all who saw it were dazzled and wondered with a great wonder. Ibby and Layla sold the rose for a splendiferous amount and built a castle on the slope of the mountains. Leofric travelled back alone to England, picking up Kronk on the way back. And the rose bloomed again the following year an ordinary flower – insofar as a rose is ever ordinary. There were no faces or messages on it.'

'What was the message?'

'Oh it was in Babylonian script. Scholars are still pondering on it even to this day. Leofric knew at once it didn't matter – the rose itself is the message.'

'So what happened to Bridget when Ibby didn't return?'

'Well now Bridget was a good sort and a sensible lady and got on with her own business. And when Leo got back he found Margarita had flounced off with her magic dress and married a baron. So Leofric – who really was a loner and enjoyed his solitary life with all his potions and with Kronk – sometimes called in on Bridget at the Trip to Jerusalem. And she filled his pipe for him and made him hot possets when he had a chill and did all kinds of warm and womanly things such as a real woman will do. . .'

'Honestly Rex, I don't believe a word. Look – the rain's stopped.'

'Be off with you – take yourself back to Moon Farm, you baggage.'

3

FARTHINGALE

When Rex left Hazel, Alan Barber found a farmhouse for her to rent on the road to Farthingale. She had sold Withy House and the new owners were camped out in the grounds, waiting to move in. Alan drove Margaret and Hazel, heavily pregnant, to see the empty house and waited in the car while the two of them went off with the key.

They passed under trees up the short front path, between a tangle of grasses and an old roofed well, opened the front door and stepped inside.

They went from room to room, throwing open doors, hearing the scurrying of field mice behind skirting boards, and breathing in the slight peppery smell, warm and musty.

'Oh look at this – the larder is a room. . .'

'Yes – ivy at the window. . .' They went wonderingly upstairs.

'What's through this door? – oh – a glory-hole. . .'

'Look – in this bedroom there are birds' nests on the window – see the little mud-houses. . .'

'Yes and. . .' They called to one another, discovering the house together.

'It's absolutely ideal for a family,' Margaret finally pronounced.

Hazel said then, 'It's lovely. But you found it and you don't have anywhere yet and you're going to have a family. You must have it.'

'Oh my dear! Look at you. Of *course* you must have it,' Margaret said warmly, pressing her arm.

The Barbers helped her move the ten miles from Withy House into Suffolk, and into their everyday orbit. Half Moon Farm, the name was hanging from the gatepost, until it finally fell off. Hazel discarded the Half bit – with the connivance of the postman, for the Half Moon pub was less than a mile away, and post did go astray.

Hazel settled in to have her baby, her mother arrived to help with the confinement, and the sunny rooms were alive with children. The utility furniture from the early days of the marriage was supplemented with pieces from her parents' home – Edwardian tub chairs which exactly fitted the rooms, with their yellowing small print wallpapers, unchanged for years.

Margaret viewed Moon Farm as a place of enchantment which sheltered Hazel and her babies, she and Alan rang every day and called most days to see if they were all right, and fetched groceries from the village two miles away. Margaret loved to call when the two rosey babies were settled for bed in their cocoons in the front bedroom. House martins had returned, busy with their nurseries too, and they came and went chattering under the eaves; summer light shone through the thin curtains, the musical box wound up and tinkling out:

> "Boys and girls come out to play
> The moon doth shine as bright as day
> Leave your beds and leave your sleep. . .'

The voices getting slower as the mechanism wound down and the babies nodded off.

The year rolled round and baby Nick's first birthday came remarkably speedily.

Rex's instinct and inclination and newer family commitments made him want to give Moon Farm a wide berth. But he couldn't help himself, he had to ring her.

'We've made it then,' he said. 'We're up there at last. This is just the beginning.' His enthusiasm was infectious and Hazel

56

knew at once he was talking about Yuri Gagarin, whizzing round the earth and looking down. The first cosmonaut. The word made him prickle and he felt elation, as though he himself were out there, up there, among the blue and all the millions and trillions of stars.

The Reverend Radice from Thankful church called, he had heard that Mrs Marlowe had a toddler and wondered about its baptism, whether she would like him to make arrangements. He was proud of his font – babies had been christened in it for five hundred years. Mrs Grove, Hazel's mother, plied him with tea and cake. He stood looking all the way down from his bulk and height to small Nick, standing firmly in his nappy and looking back with fierce blue basilisk stare.

'What is in a child's mind, I ask myself. Such very *alien* little beings, don't you find, Mrs Marlowe?'

Hazel tossed her hair scornfully and said, 'My children don't need christening.'

Mrs Grove replied warmly, 'Oh these children are very advanced you know, vicar.' And then, attempting rapprochement with one of the cloth: 'Of course, I'm not a subscriber to orthodoxy, but I do believe in the divine purposiveness of the universe,' she said, still enthusiastic into her eighties.

'Ah,' replied the Reverend Radice, imperially uncertain, putting his teacup back into its saucer.

In the midlands Jandy turned in her bed, dreaming she walked the lane from the Barbers to the Marlowes. She trod onwards, and as she walked there shone two moons in the dark heavens. She blinked, but they were still there. When she awoke she received news of this other world.

Margaret Barber to Jandy Lockhart
My dear Jandy,

Such a storm we had at the beginning of the week, the lights all off, we've been cooking on the Rayburn and lighting candles. Hazel had a big shock, she went up to see the children during the storm and there they were, all sleeping soundly. The next day she found the ends of their beds scorched where the lightning had struck in the night, and the carpet burnt. The children had slept through it all but Hazel nearly had a fit the next day. I do hope you are keeping well. Jasper is teething, poor little chap, so he isn't at his best. But he is such a joy and we are so lucky to have him.

I do hope when you come in the summer you will stay a full year, Alan thinks you ought to take your A-levels. Michael and Madeleine are coming this evening, if they can get a babysitter.

Let us know how you are.
Fondest love,
Margaret

Jandy read the news from that other world, the world of Farthingale where the babies were being reared – the precious babies sleeping unaware – it had been jeopardised but it continued.

It was twenty years since D-Day, and Farthingale was covered in triangular bits of bunting. The village hall flew the flag and a tea of sandwiches, jellies and iced cakes was laid out on trestle tables for the children.

Margaret, Hazel and Jo Perkyn did their share of cooking the cakes and Alan ferried them to their destination. That evening Hazel went to the Barbers' for supper. 'Hi folks. How were the little darlings? Did they get off without anybody being sick?' began Hazel, interrupted by Margaret bustling in with the food.

'Here we are. I did think of doing commemorative spam fritters, but thought better of it – we had quite enough of them during the War.'

'I'll say,' Hazel replied.

'On D-Day I was working as a student teacher, I'd been sent to Moss Side, it was a deprived area then. The children were given breakfast when they arrived at school, to make sure they'd had something to eat. And the smell when you walked into the classroom in the mornings – it knocked you back. Some of them hadn't changed their clothes for weeks. The deprivation seems unbelievable now. The end of the War at least finished that off.'

The other two looked up as she spoke, Alan unwrapped his napkin and Margaret nodded sympathetically. 'Come along now,' urged Hazel, 'what were you doing on D-Day?'

Margaret passed round the dish of cauliflower cheese and avoided the direct question. 'The War started on my fourteenth birthday. It overshadowed the day completely. It was just before I went back to school. Our school was evacuated to Rutland, to an old house with a ghost, so we found it quite exciting, except two of the girls didn't come back after the holidays because they were killed in an air-raid. They were sisters – Pamela and Peggy Dwyer. Their parents were in India. As we were waiting to go home that term Pam wrote in a school book, "Pamela Dwyer died of boredom on Whittlesey station while waiting for the 4.25" and then neither of them came back because they were killed,' she finished. 'She would have been a prefect next term as well,' she added inconsequentially.

'I suppose I was at school on D-Day,' said Alan slowly, 'but it wasn't particularly memorable. We were very insulated. School assembly of course always had news of old boys killed in action, but it seemed very far away. Later that year I left school and went to train with the Fleet Air Arm, in Canada. I have almost no memories of that time. We did what we had to and then it was done, as far as I was concerned,' he said.

'The relief that the War was over was the feeling I remember most.' He wasn't a person who looked back. The only photo he had was one of half a dozen of the crew on deck in bell-bottoms and hats, Alan with a debonair gesture pointing to a placard announcing "The Singing Beltones".

Much more vivid to him were the memories of going to the Tyrol afterwards, and the delight of discovering his few relations there who had been on the Other Side, and had survived. He had an awakening recognition – that proved false – that he belonged there. The air in the hills went to his head, he had never felt more excited in his life than when in the bare little castle room with its thick walls and bed and one hard chair; he looked from the tiny window down into the valley and breathed in the rarefied air. The grandeur and simplicity of it moved him deeply.

He stayed there for two years, helping with the harvests and reading poetry, grateful that he had this precious time, that he hadn't been killed and neither had they. Then he felt it was time he got something started for himself, and came back to England with ideas about the mystic land, earth yielding fruits for Man, the superiority of those who lived on the earth in a natural way.

So he left the Tyrol, taking his flaxen princess from her castle. Back in England they went looking for farms, they must stay close to the land, back to the true values. No more war or killing.

'Can we try to find Ronald Duncan?' she urged. She had read one of his books on agrarian reform. They drove to Devon, looking for him. They found him living alone, it was evening and he offered them wine. Then he invited them to see his own water pumping system, and they traipsed outside and watched the tiny man in big wellingtons proudly pumping water. He spoke of cooperative farming and they listened, spellbound, enthusiastic. The values of the peasantry would prevail. Money would be put in its place.

He was rather moved by the three youngsters – for they had taken Tony, Alan's brother. He didn't know of any land locally, but there was an agrarian commune, started by pacifists, in Norfolk. Perhaps they would like to see it?

They drove to Norfolk the next day, their world young and the War over. He thought she looked like a corn queen, with her blooming rosy skin and blonde diadem of plaits. So that was how he settled in East Anglia, and he had told Rex and Hazel of his former plans and of the golden girl, of how she had inspired him and then gone back to her husband.

Hazel pushed the supper dish at him and said, 'Rex of

course went into the Recruiting Office on the day War broke out. He was far too young, he was only thirteen. When he was fifteen he went again and told them he was eighteen.'

'Oh well, Rex would do that,' agreed Alan.

'He was so anxious to fight fascism. But I sometimes think he exaggerated some of the things that happened to him,' she continued. 'He tells one story about machine-gunning a plane that was swooping down on him on the deck of the ship – he shot the pilot close-to. And I suddenly realised – it's identical to the very scene in a film with Humphrey Bogart.' She shook her head. Alan demurred, rather shocked. Rex was a cad but he didn't lie, he didn't need to lie.

'Well Hazel,' he reproved, 'Rex and very many others like him did do those things and Humphrey Bogart didn't – he wasn't in the war.'

Margaret let her mind stray as Hazel and Alan talked on across the laden table. She had avoided Hazel's direct question. On D-Day teenage Margaret had crossed London at the height of the summer, the height of the War, alone and fearful, sent away to give birth, to keep the shame of it well away. Alert the whole time for the recently appeared doodlebugs, she carried a light suitcase and negotiated her bump, stepping out of the train into St. Pancras Station, alive with noise and steam and the smell of sulphur. Events were out of control, everything – this train journey and all that was happening, whichever way she turned. A year before, getting ready for work, Margaret and her mother heard bombers go over and they dived under the table.

The planes passed and dropped their bombs at Rolls-Royce, and then had flown low and machine-gunned everyone walking to work. Her friend in the office – Margaret too, also seventeen – had been gunned down. Margaret was in shock, and her mother wept. 'That little girl. That poor little girl – her mother's only child,' she grieved, clutching at her own Margaret. That autumn, within a month of her eighteenth birthday, Margaret had met a young American at the NAAFI van she helped with, and become pregnant. It was mad, it was unreal, but was part of the push of life.

Tipping her head, she thought she heard Jasper cry from his cot, and she left Hazel and Alan eating and talking.

'Of course we all pulled together, that was what was so good. And yet some of it brassed me off,' said Hazel, taking a roll from the plate he offered and starting to butter it. 'We had to go to Civil Defence from school in the evenings, and the very first time they formed up straightaway in a line and said Yes Sir and No Sir and you could see that for some people they couldn't wait to be told what to do. The word Sir said like that – it would stick in my throat, I couldn't use it.'

Alan laughed. 'No, well, I don't suppose you could.'

'Surely the times we are living in,' said Michael Turner later at Hamlin House, the country club they met up in, 'are the logical continuation of the great reforming forties. The country is reaping the benefit now. . .' Michael was big and tall, and always more detached than the others, he seemed to have an extra line of vision because of his height.

'Labour government of course,' swiped Hazel lightly. The men smiled back at her, taking it on the chin. Hazel was getting used now to being alone among couples, able to hold her own, more than a match for the wives in any case.

Michael and Alan had gone through school together, and had both moved to East Anglia in the early 1950s. They were members of Hamlin House and met up there once a week, sometimes taking their wives, babysitters permitting. It was a place to take visitors too, and the visitors felt they had gone somewhere special. It looked as though it had been there all century and had never changed, with its dark wood and fire and comfortable armchairs.

Alan and Michael drank beer, Margaret and Madeleine had shorts, Hazel – who hardly ever came here after Rex had left, asked for 'anything, but it must have a cherry in it', and cared less that it didn't sound sophisticated.

They fell to discussing the ludicrous length of the fashionable skirt. 'Let's face it, most women don't have legs you want to see,' said Michael.

'Oh I don't know. I mean, if they want to wear them. . .' offered Alan mildly.

'What length do you feel is most attractive?' Michael asked Hazel, as though deferring to her.

'Oh mid-calf. I remember when the New Look came in, how luxurious it felt, after six years of skimpy skirts.' Shortly they would inevitably get on to how society should be organised, and the running of schools. They were both teachers, Michael head of an English department, and he always had a regard for Hazel's opinions, whilst sharing very few of them.

Alan sat with his beer, only half-listening. He was still recovering from the sale of the farm, earlier in the year. In the autumn he would be helping Michael harvest his few acres, after school.

It was a great wonder to him now, that it had started with the intention of being a pacifist farm. Somehow the day to day tasks, ploughing and milking and sluicing, hedging, ditch-digging, not to mention plumbing and roofing, clearing the cesspit, collecting eggs, harvesting – seemed to consume all the hours in the day. With an introduction from Ronald Duncan, he was invited to look round the local community farm, he had watched them dig their shining furrows and listened as the elderly man who had founded the community explained its running, and how they had weekly meetings which all were expected to attend, to decide work and policy. The Community of Peace commune believed, he said, that capitalism was doomed by its own contradictions, the competition which gave it such unique energy would eventually destroy it. When that happened cooperatives were the answer, everyone working in harmony for the good of all. 'A responsible fellowship of workers,' he explained urgently. Young Alan had nodded, impressed by his sincerity but not much convinced that the rest of the Community were listening or reading the pamphlets, one of which he pressed into Alan's hand. 'The whole of civilisation depends on production from the land,' it read. That was more like it, Alan thought. But even if they had been more determined than they were, it was difficult. The Community of Peace had started up in the War and was still run by conscientious objectors and refugees, used to living communally on lentils and porridge, and Alan didn't see where he and Tony would find such people. He also suspected that in spite of the ideals drawn up by the founder, there was fierce friction amongst the pacifists. This was confirmed by Rex and Hazel who, supportive of the original intentions if not of the pacifism, took a keen interest.

The brothers moved into a large and draughty old farmhouse, many of the rooms shut off and inhabited by mice. On the farm were rickety barns and gates askew; hens ran with squawks from under sheds and fell flapping out of trees, rusting pitchforks lay in nettles under a hot sun. But his sense of excitement was undiminished. They could do anything.

All communities rested on trust, the Community of Peace leader had said. But the brothers didn't trust each other. The only person Alan came to trust was Tom Feetham from the village, always there when needed, often the two of them were alone in a dismal autumn field, up to their ankles in water, trying to find sugar-beet in a swirl of mud. Frost was the worst, if it got into their fingers. And in the summer he'd ask, 'What do you think Tom? Is it ready?' Tom would squint his dark blue eyes against the sun, surveying the corn, and nod or shake his head. Tom's face tanned and leathery, Alan's harvest jumper full of holes and corn dust, dust in his hair and beard, the sun baking. . . their throats tickling. . . Margaret appearing at the edge of the meadow with flasks and food.

His brother Tony, although not a slacker about work, was certainly a backslider about their original plans and soon professed himself keen on making a big profit. He broke away and set up broiler houses. There wasn't a squawking hen about the place, they were all inside the big hangars which Tony had bought cheaply from a sale and erected in a field. Alan carried on with his work, he made new barns for the cows himself, and there was a shiny new dairy amongst the mud-tracks. He always felt confident when something real and physical was involved.

So from the pacifist intentions all that was left was a largely unread pamphlet and the splendid milking parlour and new barns. And now even they were gone.

'Cheer up,' said Michael, breaking into his reverie, 'and drink up. It's my round.' He went to the bar and ordered and brought the drinks with surprising rapidity. It was a slack night at Hamlin House. He placed half a bitter before Alan and shorts for Madeleine and Margaret. With a big smile he put a martini with a cherry before Hazel.

'And how's Rex these days – what's he up to?' he asked.

The conversation always got round to Rex eventually.

In his study Rex tried to work on his latest book, whilst the smells of dinner floated up the stairs. Gillian would be bringing it soon on a tray, so he must finish his daily stint, not let his attention wander. She was a wonderful cook, the meal would be worth the eating. He had learned to cook at sea, had taught Hazel to cook, for she had no clue at all in the kitchen when they had first married, an aristocratic lift of the head met any remark of his mother's about whether she could cook. She had made him wait for sex, he didn't think anything of it, he was only eighteen and there were other things more immediately important.

The sea – the sea all around, the sea everywhere. 'He ran away to sea'. When he was growing up that's what naughty boys did, boys in old tales, boys in the long ago.

There was a strange wobbling feeling he had had when the ship had been at sea for more than a couple of days and had not seen anything other than sea and sky. He supposed it must be akin to the state the old tars had been in when they started seeing mermaids – they had to pull something out of themselves to keep going. Maybe his days at sea were why he felt so immediately at home when they moved to Norfolk – the mist swirling over the land at daybreak reminded him of the turning ocean, and the vast expanse of sky, sky as a presence, sky stretching to infinity. You can't forget the sky in East Anglia.

With the war had come the loss of certainty. But perhaps

that doesn't matter too much to the young. One looked differently at people, for who would be alive the next week, the next day? 'Make Love Not War' they said now. It was wrong, you had to make war in order to make love, any animal could tell you that.

He had been a radio operator on a tug ferrying concrete blocks to make a harbour for the D-Day landings. The radio was crackling like crazy and when one of the ships was summoned back to Britain neither he nor the radio operators on the other ship could make out which of them was being named.

He had pulled off his ear-phones and hung over the deck shouting to the sailors on the other ship, who hollered back they didn't know either. They couldn't hang about – war was like that – and with gusto they decided to race for it. The ship that made the harbour mouth would be the one that went home. They geared up for the race and steamed ahead, but the other destroyer pipped them to the post. But German mines had been laid in the harbour entrance and the crew of his ship watched as the other went up, leaning over the side they saw the bodies in the water of the chaps they had just called to, blood and bodies and water. . .

He moved his pens as he was thinking, disturbing a boat left by his toddler son. It made him think of the playroom at Withy House and small Shane, playing with a toy tug. It was strange to Rex to see him, just a very few years after the War. He had looked at the tiny plastic men that were the crew, at the paper Victory flag, and saw his own history encapsulated in his son's toys, to be picked up or discarded. But as he grew Shane was only interested in space ships, not the terrestrial kind. Rex was quite in awe of him already. He handled the bright plastic boat and thought of his little son, being put to bed now and so demanding, so dependent. Rex was naturally tender towards the young. This tenderness he felt was thwarted when he went to Moon Farm, each time ready to make himself available to his children, in every way – to sympathise, assist, advise. . . Only to find them not quite as he remembered; seemingly hostile.

Gillian was blonde and soft and yielding. Quite different from Hazel. With her he had shared that comradeship that had attracted him, and that had finally proved irksome. Sometimes he missed it. She was a few years older than he, socially confident and yet when the masks were off heartbreakingly dependent upon him as a woman. He thought of that insouciance the wartime women had, the camaraderie and jokes, the neat factory turbans or bright little hats at an angle.

Rex touched the work he was supposed to be doing, toying over the pages and recapping.

'Hear me, dirt man. When your dirt woman brings forth her third child, her life is forfeit, as you well know. . .' Qermys heard the alien male, chief of the Spotless Ones, those who dominated their lives and made them to bring forth young and to work, and to suppress their true human feelings to fit with the whim of the Spotless. Only the Spotless Ones were considered worthy of Knowledge, of Art, of Science. Thus it was on this Other Planet, in this world other than Earth. Qermys felt the pull of earth all the more for being estranged from it, and his heart beat and thundered with resentment that his woman should be so treated. . .'

Rex hovered over the manuscript. He supposed it could be said he had sublimated his class feelings in his work, but he had wanted to embrace the generality, to cast wide the net of his concern over all, not just his own class. In the War he had mixed with officers and the middle class, and while some of them undoubtedly had been snotty, many were most agreeable sorts, they were all in it together. He didn't see himself or his parents as class victims, and it seemed demeaning to treat them as such. Wanting to write true yet wanting to avoid the negative aspects of the class situation, he at first looked outward to the Soviet Union. Then to big tumultuous America. He framed his reference points always as far as possible. Finally, space seemed as far as you could go.

When teaching he had shared a staff room with colleagues who considered working class children laboured under a grievous injustice, and Rex saw it was so. He felt part of the new mood that indicated all children should share in what was there, should reap the benefit of the War. Why else would their parents have fought it? Even when he was great friends with Harry and nominally a member of the Communist Party Rex felt detached, as though some important part of him was untouched. Lawrence was his hero – a working class man who had transcended class. Rex didn't want to be trapped in his background, he admired Lawrence for escaping his class, escaping his country.

The War, the fighting and uncertainty over, Nazism defeated, he and Hazel were going to rear a fine troop of golden young.

Aged six, Judy the little black spaniel suddenly presented the Barbers with ten puppies. Four died, Hazel had one, and so did Tom Feetham in the village. Barny begged and begged his mother, but she said no. The Turners already had a dog and the Warrenders didn't want one. 'You palmed a kitten off onto us not so long ago,' Jon pointed out. The Barbers kept one, and the McGeehans in the next farm said they would have two.

'I should jolly well think so too, it was their dog who was responsible,' said Margaret indignantly. 'Judy didn't want them, did you dear?' It was horribly true. The little spaniel cast paranoid looks over her shoulder at the heap of scrapping yelping pups, and left the room.

Egged on by a giggling Margaret and Hazel, Alan rang the local US airbase. 'Hello. My name is Alan Barber, I had a spaniel bitch from your base, and she's just given birth to ten pups. Would you be interested in having one?'

He covered the mouthpiece. 'He's gone to ask. You note I forbore to mention we had her from them four years ago.'

'Well, if they want to do their bit for the Transatlantic Alliance. . .' pointed out Hazel.

'They ought to do the Decent Thing,' finished Margaret, and they snickered away together.

'Hello. Yes. Yes. . .' Alan gave a thumbs up sign to the females. 'They should be ready in about ten to twelve weeks. . .'

The Marlowe children named their pup Spot, although no spots were to be seen on him.

Between the Barbers bottle-feeding, and one of the cats who had never been allowed to keep her kittens, the pups were reared. The cat, adult but very small, kept getting in with the pups and as they grew they licked and chewed her and knocked her over and nipped her ears, and poor Poppy purred, blissfully happy and proud of them.

Margaret Barber to Jandy Lockhart

My Dear Jandy,

We are both so pleased you have decided to take up Alan's offer. It will be good for you to be down here and to take your exams, and you can look after the chickens at the same time, they will arrive soon, I have been out with Barny building the hen houses at the top of the garden. We started from scratch with twigs, and built them up in triangles, like wigwams. I feel quite proud of them and only hope the hens appreciate them! Jasper is a little scamp, and very much looking forward to seeing his aunty. I feel so blessed to have such a loving husband and a delightful baby boy. Hazel too is much looking forward to seeing you, she anticipates you will be going there quite a lot. In fact, if you come mid-August we will be in Italy, so you can stay at Moon Farm, and we'll see you when we get back in September. We already planned this trip but I know you love to stay at Moon Farm so it has worked out very well.

See you quite soon.

Our love to you,

Margaret

So Jandy packed her bags for a year instead of for the summer and boarded the train, waving goodbye to Andrew her boyfriend and promising to write.

The journey was long and cross country, it was a journey she had made every summer since Margaret married. The train rocked in its own rhythm through the flat land of fields, she ate her sandwiches and leaned forward to see Ely cathedral rising out of the fen mists like a mediaeval fairy palace, brilliant in the sun, as though Time had parted and she was seeing it as it was first built.

She arrived in St. Edfric's and for the first time there was no one to meet her and she went off to find the bus. She stepped from the bus and walked with her suitcases down the long Farthingale road from Thankful. Fortunately Moon Farm was nearer by two miles than Windy Ridge, and she bucked up when the barns and gables of the house came into view. A whole month here with Hazel and the Marlowes. She couldn't think of anything more delightful. She was looking forward to the year ahead too, although sorry to leave Nottingham which was livelier than ever, the Tory government was in crisis. But her marxist group had advised her to go.

Farthingale seemed to exist out of Time, as though by now it had abstracted from history, which had left its mark but no longer passed by there. Farthingale village street ran along and was shared with Farthingale Inferior and Weston – the same main street for three villages. Honey Weston was three miles away from Thankful.

Thankful was named so after the Great War, when all of its sons returned from the faraway mud and guns. The parish council had met and, so momentous was this good fortune felt to be (there were only thirty-one villages in the land where this occurred) that a name change to commemorate it was felt to be in order. Before that, the village was known as Hipton, presumably from the great profusion of hips in the wild old hedgerows.

Set back from the village street was the small church – Norman flint upon Saxon foundations. The original Saxon tower had been the place of refuge to where the villagers had fled when the Danes arrived to kill and pillage. This had been rebuilt in Norman times, and a small church added. The font, of which the Reverend Radice was so fond, stood at the back with its panels of stone foliage, interspersed with strange beasts – birds and lions.

As the Reverend Radice opened the pages of the Bible on

the wooden lectern, and slotted the hymn numbers for the evening service into the board behind the pulpit, he was not confident this church would be preserved. This made him sad, for it was his favourite. All was bare here, except for the font and an unknown knight with chipped fingers and his lady, in butterfly head-dress, entombed at the side. The walls were whitewashed and stark. Yet he preferred this small church to any other he had known. Farthingale Church, not big, was about twice the size of this one, it had dainty tracery and glistening gilt and red effigies of Sir Roger Bigod and Alice his wyffe, a trail of their infants behind them, ruffed and speaking to their Maker.

Looking out of the bare windows onto grass he was aware of the crumbling of the churches and the reluctance to spend money restoring every last one, and he feared desuetude loomed for the butterfly lady and the sleeping knight. The knight was anonymous and sandstone, he had returned from crusading when the monks at Ely were toiling away at their manuscripts. It was the Reverend Radice's fanciful notion that to those monks these small flint churches were like space-ships are to us now, the containers of Man's knowledge, hurtling away into the cruel future.

He smiled at that old idea. The future is always cruel, by its very nature. He took a last look round the little church, adjusted a hassock, picked up a hair-ribbon dropped by the Sunday School. In our innocence we have supplanted the generations before, the future has arrived, it is here. This is the Future.

In Moon Farm kitchen Hazel was cooking a meal and small Hebe was taking the matryoshka doll to pieces, mother out of mother out of mother, bright red and dolly faced. The child seemed mesmerised by the repetition and innocently plundered the future, her fingers clutched about the wood, her expression intent and frowning. Hazel's sister Helen had brought it back from the Soviet Union. Helen was ten years older than Hazel and Hazel had grown up rather awed by her.

Unmarried, she was into everything, had gone off to see the Passion at Oberammergau when everybody knew the War was in the offing; she dressed in rather racy tweeds, flirted with communism, and had recently become a headmistress. Hazel was still a little intimidated by her two elder sisters, who were young women when she was a child.

Through the kitchen window she viewed Shane with Dale Perkyn, playing rounders alongside Lynnet and Philip, one of the children of her other sister Ann. Philip was almost a summer fixture. He was under a psychiatrist, and every so often when he was particularly stressed the pupil in one of his eyes went wonky. When that happened he was packed off to Moon Farm, as being in the country and calm, and eventually the eye righted itself. Philip looked after the hens and was writing a book. 'What is it about?' people asked.

'Oh God. It's so long I've forgotten the beginning,' Philip replied gloomily.

The doorbell rang, Hazel turned down the gas under the potatoes, and Jandy staggered through into the hall with cases.

In the early September heat rain splattered against window panes and thunder rumbled and barked across the flat land and fetched down electricity wires.

Hazel and Jandy were in Moon Farm kitchen, polishing the brass paraffin lamps. In the early years of their marriage Hazel and Rex had found them in the attics at Withy House, left there by Katherine Mansfield and Middleton Murry.

'The red shades were Rex's idea. He suddenly had a thing about red, he couldn't get enough of it, and that's when this paterfamilias thing seemed to take over him,' said Hazel, rubbing hard with the cloth, to bring up the shine. 'The red shades do give off a very sexual ambiance. Rex would write under these lamps, we thought the spirit of Mansfield and Murry was good luck for us, and I was pregnant time after time.'

'But Katherine Mansfield rejected the maternal role laid down for females,' objected Jandy, also rubbing hard, as though trying to bring forth a genie.

'Oh well, I don't know – we thought they brought us luck – something seemed to emanate from the lamps. But the red light is too powerful, too disturbing.'

'You might change the shades,' suggested Jandy.

But Hazel said hastily, 'Oh we can't change them now, it's far too late.'

When Lynnet came from school, shaking herself dry in the kitchen, Jandy said to her, 'Honestly – Hazel has been complaining about the red lampshades, but when I suggested changing them, she wouldn't.'

'Oh I know,' agreed Lynnet, 'it's all the fault of the lampshades she's had five children. She complains, but underneath she's pleased about it.'

'Well I don't come from round here, I think they're all crackers.'

Lynnet laughed, as Jandy continued.

'No but not just Hazel, Margaret and Alan too.'

'Oh I know, they're absolutely crackers,' agreed Lynnet.

'They keep Gaudier-Brzeskas under the bed.'

'Well that doesn't surprise me,' answered Lynnet in her grandest tone. She hadn't the slightest idea what these were, but believed in keeping her end up.

The next day Hazel and Jandy sat out in the garden. 'Let's go through your button box,' pleaded Jandy, planting the elderly tin on the grass in front of Hazel.

'Well now, that button's from a maternity dress. . .' began Hazel. 'In the afternoons Rex and myself would wander through Thelnetham churchyard when I was pregnant, looking at the names on the tombs of the people who had been born and had died. Rex's work was going well and I felt full of life and hope. It was a good time for us. We picked the coming baby's name from the tombstones – Simon or Sarah. But one of the stones said "I hold you prisoner in Love's chains". What a negation of true love,' Hazel said passionately. 'We both thought so. . .' Jandy nodded encouragingly as Hazel continued. 'I never regretted having the children. Women exist in the byways of history, but those are often pleasant places to

73

d

be, you know. A life can be fulfilling without overweening ambition pinching all the time.'

Hazel was alone – the children in bed, Lynnet in her room listening to pop records, and Alan had collected Jandy. Still in the wake of her earlier reminiscences she recalled one particular day at Withy House, heavy with summer, she and Rex had taken their habitual afternoon stroll through the churchyard, she heavy with the coming birth, 'great with child' as the sixteenth century scribes had translated the old words. Wandering between the ranks of graves they had felt close to the turn of the earth, part of its blooming and its utter victims. Once back home she had made a meal – a simple stew, for they had little money – and put small Lynnet to bed, whilst Rex worked under the old brass lamps they believed brought them luck. She waited until she heard his final slower tap-tap, preparatory to replacing the cover on the typewriter, before putting out the food.

He came down the dark old stairs, triumphant. He had worked well. After they had eaten he showed her what he had written. He put his hands on her swelling belly as she read, and buried his face in her breasts, already beginning to leak.

And what she read was a story of their house, the home that sheltered them with its ancient timber and brick, its pantiles and thatched roof and studded doors. It was in ruins, in the story, brick fell from brick, only the battered chimney-stacks were left, and the memory of the people who had lived there swirled about between the weeds and the ruins. 'It's good,' she said. 'Very good, my precious love.' He had reached for her and in anguish and despair and triumph they made love on the floor.

Afterwards they held hands and wandered about outside in the dark and watched their house, a moon-washed Elizabethan cottage in the stillness, knowing themselves fleeting and mortal.

'Is it true?' they whispered to one another. 'Is this dream really ours?' The walls had sheltered folk when Elizabeth Tudor reigned in all her splendour – homely stalwart folk, who had just as many dreams and fears as they did. Then

74

suddenly they were between the walls like phantoms themselves, overwhelmed with the past.

When she left she did so because Rex had left and, in spite of the children and the coming baby, it was an empty house to her. She could no longer sustain it. That was the reason she had sold it and not because of the debts. Hazel knew now her big mistake had been leaving Withy House. She had begun to understand that, belying appearances, Rex felt he had been the deserted one. Her mistake devastated her, but also gave her magic and confidence.

Jandy watched out of the window as each evening darkened early – an unusual occurrence, for Farthingale was in perpetual summer to her. Neither Lynnet nor Jandy were old enough to vote in the General Election of October 1964, but they tramped round Farthingale and Farthingale Inferior, campaigning for a Labour victory. The old days should be back again, of the Attlee government and nationalisation and the NHS. Fair shares for all. ('To think we walked our socks off for Labour and got Wilson,' Lynnet said to Jandy years later, both sipping Baileys. 'Yes. And eventually we got Thatcher,' answered Jandy, and they laughed ruefully.)

Jandy was a teller at the village school wearing a big red rosette and holding a card to mark down the number of people coming in. Alan called to pick her up in his farm van, decked about with blue rosettes and a picture of Eldon Griffiths, the local Tory MP. As the van clacketed slowly through the village it was hailed by the Reverend Radice, on his way to Thankful.

'Ahoy there!' he waved at them with his black umbrella. 'Have you room for a non-practising Liberal? – no, no, I can ride on the back,' he said, declining a seat and clambering up into the cart and standing there massive in his cassock as the van trundled on its way.

Lynnet canvassed Dr Barber, calling forth Alan's indignation. Margaret stoutly stuck up for her. 'Darling I don't see how Lynnet can be expected to know Daddy doesn't vote Labour. How would she know? She's only a schoolgirl.'

'She probably thought she could convert him,' added Jandy.

'Oh *really*,' said an exasperated Alan.

'Females have a cranial capacity 125cc less than men's – never forget,' Lynnet quoted her father to Jandy on one of their missionary treks round the village.

'Yes. And never forget girls can read too,' replied Jandy.

'Never forget – girls can read too,' the Judge had warned at the Lady Chatterley trial – a statement which caused ripples of merriment in Moon Farm quarters.

They were thrilled about the new government, even though it had a majority of four. Times were going to change now.

Councillor Mike Sharpe to the *East Anglian Times*

Dear Citizens,

It was agreed in Council that Thomas Paine's life be celebrated in the place of his birth by erecting a statue of him in the main street. This would be a fitting tribute to a man whose ideas were so powerful they contributed to the American and French revolutions. Indeed, he was a signatory to both those constitutions, which he had helped to draft. It would be of interest to our American and French visitors, and show that the cause of Freedom is not forgotten.

> Yours faithfully,
> Mike Sharpe

Major A.P.C. Gadsby-Smith to the *East Anglian Times*

Sirs,

I feel called upon to express my dismay, not to say anger, at the proposal by Thetford District Council to put up a statue to the arch-traitor Thomas Paine. A corset-maker of that town, he made a thorough nuisance of himself here, then took off to France and ended up in America. In both places he sided with the enemy against the British. He was a viper in the nest of the land that nurtured him. Why bother to have an Army to fight these people and then mollycoddle them in our midst? Have we

76

come to such a pass?
I remain, sir, yours truly,
    A.P.C. Gadsby-Smith (Major-ret'd)

Etc., etc., this correspondence continued interminably, decorating the pages of the *East Anglian Times* each week that year, Dr Barber and Margaret mulling them over non-committally and reading bits out to one another.

It was true about the Gaudier-Brzeskas. Margaret led the way into the bedroom and pulled them from under the bed.

'I don't understand it,' she frowned, puzzling and shaking her head over the thin muscular torsos. 'Why don't you hang them up for Godsake, that's what people do with pictures.'

Margaret was shocked. 'We can't do that, they're worth pots of money. Anyway, I don't like them, I prefer Daddy's paintings. Just a few lines on a piece of paper – they haven't even got heads – and if we sold them we could buy expensive cars with the proceeds.'

'Yeh well, that's Art for you,' responded Jandy, delighted there was another thing in the world that foxed Margaret.

In the New Year the Marlowes went down with 'flu, prostrate on beds. Jandy stayed over and made meals and took them up on trays, swapping over with Lynnet when she came from school to take over the nursing. 'How are they?'

'They're all asleep at the moment.'

She left it to Lynnet, turning the corner into the Thelnetham road, and a sudden dense white fog descended on everything, she couldn't even see her feet, the lane blocked out, the way back non-existent, and two miles to go. She blundered on hopelessly and then became aware of someone else close by in the nothingness, and uttered a little scream. It was Rip, the farm Alsatian, his nose suddenly touched her hand and she made an enormous fuss of him, she was so pleased. She followed him, keeping hold of his collar through the thick vapour. It was uncanny and disorienting, the fog so dense there was no feeling of being anywhere on a map. He went his own way, they seemed to be in wet muddy fields. 'Oh God, where are we going Rip you ole bugger?' But suddenly out of nothing they came up against Windy Ridge front doorstep.

'Well done boy,' said Margaret when she heard how he and Jandy had got back.

Rip was an old moth-eaten Alsatian, still full of beans but with a sad expression on his face. He belonged to Alan's brother Tony, and when younger he had had an awful reputation for killing cats and savaging neighbours. There was one family he particularly detested, he knocked them off their bikes and lay in wait to corner them in lanes. He had twice been up before the magistrates but it was a farming area and the cases were discharged, after Tony paid a fine.

'He's an old sinner, I'm afraid,' said Dr Barber.

He seemed to have calmed down now, he roamed the farm unchecked, and when Judy had neglected her puppies Rip was kindly towards them, he gave them the odd lick and watched them play together, and sat wagging his tail slowly for them to jump on.

Then Dr Barber went off to T.S.Eliot's memorial service in Westminster Abbey. When he returned to Farthingale they all leaned forward to hear about it.

'It was interesting, they read some of his poetry. Afterwards I went with Olga and Ezra to have tea at the Tate. They do things very well there. Ezra didn't open his mouth the entire time, he sat there like a stone. Olga of course more than made up for it, she never shuts up. But I don't see' – his voice became uncharacteristically peeved – 'why anyone would travel all that way and then never speak, not even to say hello or goodbye good-riddance.'

In the evening Hazel read from the *Four Quartets* to Lynnet and Jandy, under the red lamps.

The telephone sang out in Moon Farm sitting room, and Hebe put down the blue plastic pig she was dressing and answered it. Crashing the receiver down onto its side, she rushed into the kitchen and announced importantly, 'It's Daddy on the phone.'

Hazel dried her hands quickly and hurried through. 'Hello?'

'Oh hello. Our daughter doesn't have any regard for my ears when she bangs the receiver down, you might point out to her.'

'Oh. Yes.'

'Did the cheque arrive?'

'Yes. Yes. . . thank you. How's things?'

'I've called you about something important we need to discuss. I have the chance of a great big house in the country. It's quite splendid – you'd love it, the children would love it. There's one snag.'

'Oh?'

'It will only be possible if we all live there. I can't afford to maintain two separate households. There's plenty of room, nobody will be under anybody's feet, and it will be good for the kids, to get to know one another and play together.'

'Well you've rather sprung this on me,' she protested.

'Yes I know. I'm sorry. I've been thinking about it for some time and the opportunity arose. It would be madness not to take it. But it all depends on you. It's a great place. You'll love it. You must see it before you decide.'

'Well. . . I don't know. Apart from other considerations Rex, two women sharing a kitchen can lead to all kinds of friction. . .' She didn't add 'let alone a man'.

'We can sort all these things out,' he urged. 'The place is vast, you don't need to share a kitchen. All these things can be resolved in practice, that's the best way to solve anything. Don't make your mind up now. Think on it. And I'll arrange to take you down there. It will be good for the children to be out in the country. . .'

'Well these children are in the country now,' she pointed out.

'Look,' he said desperately, 'all these payments going in different directions are bleeding me dry, and if we work together we can solve this one. . . without preconceptions of what human beings ought to do.'

'Yes,' she said uncertainly. 'I'll sleep on it.'

Hazel put down the receiver and took a big sigh.

Lynnet said she didn't mind, Jandy was militantly in favour. 'Gosh Hazel, that's ripping, you'll be part of new life forms.'

'Oh Hazel *no* – absolutely not. The cheek of the man!' said Margaret.

'Well I don't know. I'm giving it careful consideration,' replied Hazel. 'There are some advantages.'

'I should have thought you had had enough trouble with him, my dear, without volunteering for any more,' answered Alan.

'Now Jandy, when you go to Moon Farm will you please calm down and modify your language. Mrs Grove is there, Hazel's mother, she's in her eighties and she is so very very sweet,' instructed Margaret.

Mrs Grove amazed them all by being in favour of Rex's proposal. 'Oh yes. Of course at one time it was quite the thing, when I was a girl. I was at the Free Trade Hall you know when Sylvia Pankhurst announced she had contracted a free union, and was now with child,' said Mrs Grove, her voice slowing down and taking on the cadences of the announcement. '*She* wasn't going to be bound by the shackles of patriarchy. Oh no.'

Hazel looked amused and patient and said nothing. 'Marriage of course is legalised prostitution – that's what George Bernard Shaw thought, and who are we to disagree with him?' she continued. 'Yes, well as an erstwhile legalised prostitute, I'll go and get the tea on. And two women readily available to one man will surely reinforce patriarchy,' Hazel bounced back.

In the kitchen Jandy helped Hazel cut sandwiches and remarked approvingly, 'Your mother's very progressive, isn't she?'

'That's claptrap,' steamed back Hazel. 'Absolute Edwardian claptrap. Just as though Mother would have allowed Pop to bring another woman into the family home – she would have soon read the Riot Act to him if he'd done that.'

Jandy saw any chance of Hazel becoming part of a communal household was entirely scotched by her mother's vigorous approval of it.

'Don't put so much potted beef on, there's only just enough to go round,' instructed Hazel.

'I thought it would be better to put lots on some and none on others – All or Nothing, you know, rather than scraping.'

'Yes dear, I take your point but I don't think those getting the nothing will be too chuffed.'

'Well I don't mind having nothing.'

'I'll hold you to that if we run short,' laughed Hazel.

She sent Jandy in with the sandwiches, took a quick look round the kitchen, and put the butter in the 'fridge. Her mother was an ideal grandmother. She revelled in the children and didn't interfere, but Hazel wasn't close to her in an intimate daughterly way. Her mother had been ill when Hazel was a child and she had been sent away for two years to spinster aunts, where she had acquired a detached way of regarding her parents. The aunts spoke freely of her parents' foolishness in one way or another, so she never really fell back into the role of child when she returned home. Both she and her sister Ann had had five children, so that's how much notice they had taken of their mother's views on birth control. The life she and Rex had made together was everything to Hazel. Yet she still felt an allegiance to Manchester. Although they had lived in the suburbs, she and her sisters were brought up with an understanding of the grandeur of Manchester, its industry and grime, and great sense of purpose. The smoky city with its immense bonded warehouses, hidden corners, imposing Town Hall, street upon street of factories, which had nurtured Engels and his stocking mills, relentlessly turning. Who was it who said, 'Without Manchester, 1917 in Russia would never have happened'?

The young suffragette Bess Acre, her mother, still exercised a hold on Hazel's imagination. Small and lively, the daughter of a prosperous pawn-broker, she had grown up in Cheetham Hill. But when she had seen the poorest areas of the city, where her father had his shop, she cried out that people shouldn't live like this, they should be helped. Her militant youth gone, Bess had stayed warm-hearted and concerned, and Hazel somewhat reluctantly admired her, although she had been pleased to turn from all this concern and fall into the arms of Rex, who had grasp of a fiercer reality. They both agreed – the country was the only civilised place to live and rear children.

Hazel always ended the children's pre-bed playtimes with a fearsome thing called a mummybeat. Hebe and Nick would fly at her, shrieking and pummelling. Alan, calling there on such an occasion, was horrified and remonstrated with her. 'I'm concerned Hazel that they will hurt you. They're far too big now to be so boisterous.'

'Really! Those children are the absolute end,' he said when he arrived home. Margaret laughed.

A fierce verbal disciplinarian before his marriage, Alan mellowed after Jasper was born. This was mostly due to natural paternal affection, and partly to Margaret's attitude. She always supported her husband, but was liable to suddenly change allegiance on the subject of child-rearing.

At some misdemeanor of Nick's, Alan had suggested a good smack. Margaret was horrified. 'Darling, no.'

'No darling?'

'No darling,' she said firmly. 'I'm with Hazel on this one.' Hazel smiled. They were Dr Spock mothers, they both had his battered paperback manual to hand in their respective sitting rooms.

Alan looked from woman to woman, aware they were in league, beyond the mereness of words, past his comprehension. He saw he was defeated before he started, by something female and unquantifiable, and he subsided.

"The Mothers, the Mothers, how ghostly does it sound."

When Hazel finally decided against Rex's one house suggestion, he held up the monthly cheque for longer and longer each time, so she was forced to ring him and – in her words – 'beg for it.' As Nick was now four, she decided to return to teaching and take him to school along with her. Jandy would do light housework in the mornings and Hazel would pay her a small wage and help her with lessons two evenings a week.

So Hazel began teaching again at Farthingale Primary and

that year Jandy kept house, messed up the cookery and didn't dust the furniture, reluctantly collected eggs from under the indignant hens and scrapped with small Hebe over hair brushing. She accidentally dyed all their clothes pink, unaware the old red dressing gown that terminated its existence in Nick's possession lurked in the secret deeps of the chuntering machine, and Hazel had come home from school to find a line of rosey washing waving gaily in the breeze.

Hazel put in a mitigatory plea about the hair brushing. 'You see, her head is so tender, it hurts her so much – mine was the same,' she pleaded, while Jandy looked coldly at both of them.

'Well I'll try to be gentle. But if I have any more fuss Hebe you'll go to school with your hair unbrushed. I don't care.'

'You ought to take the scissors to it,' put in Lynnet, and the child started shrieking.

Margaret was still having trouble with the rash on her finger, she itched and worried at it. Dr Barber prescribed cream but it didn't seem to work.

At his most priapic Rex found Hazel's fidelity a source of pride and irritation. In one of his books he had based a character on her and had written she was 'so adamantly virtuous the Andronicii would have been proud to claim her as their own'. But he had reluctantly scrapped it. Not because it wasn't true, but it didn't conjure Hazel as she was, as he had known her – with the wind in her hair, her eyes looking over the heather of the Derbyshire moors towards the sun as it rose; her fierce instincts. It was Rex who had left, yet he couldn't shake off an injured feeling that when he at last began to have some success she had turned against him.

They spoke more frequently on the telephone now, and she suddenly seemed to have a great need of him. Early in the year they held a winter reconciliation party, Hazel aglow in a pale blue knitted dress, pinning on a brooch, a marcasite sheathed scimitar, its silvery chain swinging. They asked all their friends from the old days. Margaret and Alan refused to go, as did Madeleine. 'Not when I think 'ow 'e left 'er – ze state she was in – she 'ad to pump 'er own water. Michael, my Englishman, I can't tell 'im what to do – 'e is going.'

'Absolutely not,' agreed Margaret forcefully.

Jandy, to her secret indignation, wasn't asked.

If there was a chance of Hazel and Rex getting together again for good that chance was considerably diminished when their friends ostracised Rex. Hazel was at her snootiest. 'What I find totally risible is the amount of sanctimonious drivel coming out. All of them at one time have led morally dubious lives, and now they're sitting in judgment on Rex. Michael came, he brought a bottle and he is amazingly good company. But no one else came and you can't have a party when one person turns up.'

The world of the Barbers and the Marlowes was seemingly threatened frequently by all sorts of disagreements, but these actually strengthened it as immunisation strengthens the body against hostile forces. But this time Hazel was so angry she found it hard to forgive them. But in the course of time she and Rex quarrelled again and the world of Farthingale was still there, to fall back into. The second greater jeopardisation didn't come until much later.

Margaret in her kitchen examined the red blobs on her finger. She had never worn rings before her marriage. The engagement had been brief and the ring no problem. When she was pregnant in the War she had worn a ring, for decency's sake. But once back home with her mother she removed the cheap rolled gold band, held it in her hand, surveyed its circle, with an air putting it on again as a try-out. Then with relief casting it off for good.

Pulling herself from the treacle of sleep, Jandy became aware of Hazel's absence in the bed, and she waited for her to rush back in from the bathroom to the mirror, lift the big puff on the dressing table, her face suddenly lost in a cloud of powder. Each morning she raised herself on one arm, in wait for that special moment when from the fragrant dust Hazel's features and the blue lights of her eyes returned.

The breakfast table, always laid out the night before to save time in the morning – plain white china, toast rack that ensured the toast was crisp and stone cold by the time it was eaten but was a little weakness of Hazel's; the lazy Susan with its burden of honey and condiments and always Roses lime marmalade. Small Nick laboured at the table to put the butter on top of the marmalade, he said it tasted nicer. Hebe was fractious usually, Shane smiling and abstracted, Hazel sorting dinner money or fresh clothes.

Lynnet went off first on her bike, the pink witch that she threw into the ditch at the bus-stop, before mounting the stairs and greeting Basil, the bus-driver. Hazel went next, with Nick, because they had to walk the two miles to Farthingale Inferior, to the Infants and Juniors. Shane and Hebe left last of all, they went to the village school in Thankful, half a mile away in the other direction.

When everyone had gone Jandy walked over the house, picking up the discarded nightclothes and clearing the breakfast pots, and if it was fine taking Spotty out to his pen. She made the beds, wiped the windowsills – if she remembered – with a damp cloth, scoured the bath, dusted the dish into which Hazel dropped her watch. Moon Farm lay under her hands. From Lynnet's room she watched the mist over the corn rise and slowly disperse, the road alongside running into the sky.

Then she went over the house with the vacuum cleaner. In the children's rooms Tyrannosaurus Rex reared up on the wall, light came in through the tiny squares in the upper part of the Edwardian windows. On the little mantel were Hebe's shell boxes, made with shells collected from Dunwich each summer. The musical box was high on a cupboard, only wound at bedtimes. Hebe's hair was knotted in the mornings because when the tinkle had died away she continued singing, she sang herself to sleep, rocking her head from side to side on the pillow in tune.

Shane's room was locked like a Victorian papa's room full of secrets – chemicals and bottles and potions. Hazel's room faced onto the garden and across the fields to the Perkyns' thatched cottage. Outside the crusted mud nests at the top of the windows, deserted now until late spring and the return of the house-martins.

She dusted the desk, with its blotter and pens and manuscripts. Hazel was always writing stories. A charcoal etching of Rex as a Byronic young poet presided on the wall above.

In the larder apples from the trees outside lay in rows, packed round in newspaper, stored for the winter.

Emptying the vacuum cleaner and cleaning the porridge saucepan were her least favourite tasks, otherwise she got on pretty well.

Hebe and Nick went down with measles and when they were convalescing Jandy stayed all day to look after them. This meant playing card games or sometimes refereeing scraps. She read them an American story by Max Eastman beginning "Who are you? You do not live on your own on a desert island, you have parents and friends, you live in a society of other people. . ."

'*And* Solomon Snail,' put in Nick. Hazel traditionally finished each meal apart from weekday breakfast with a Solomon Snail story and when she looked after the children Jandy had to tell one too.

Rex's Solomon the King, possessor of Wisdom and a thousand wives, became at Moon Farm Solomon the little boy, getting into a pickle in every story and being put right by Big Sister Sheba. He was fantastically popular. 'Solomon Snail – *y-e-e-e-e-es*,' thumped the children on the table with their fists, clutching cutlery.

'We have a popular uprising on our hands,' laughed Hazel one day, as they demanded:

'Solomon Snail, Solomon Snail, Solomon Snail,' because they hadn't had their story.

They both drew him as a little boy with antennae and a whorl on his back like a rucksack. He carried it round with him because he was at home everywhere in the world. Eventually

Jandy learned to forestall the demand by saying 'Now who's going to tell the Solomon Snail story?', and the children were more than capable.

'Don't worry Jandy, you're a good cooker. She's a good cooker, isn't she Hebe?' said small Nick, when Jandy flapped over making their meals. Then: 'Tell us about when Hebe was a baby,' he demanded.

'Well, when Hebe was a baby you all lived at Withy House, Rex drove a red cadillac and Hazel was pregnant with you. . .' – this image always made Nick look replete with satisfaction.

Shane somehow wasn't quite under her jurisdiction, although he was only ten. Named after the man who rode alone into the Golden West, he had been alone with his potions since the age of eight, and was eminently sensible. With his raggy fair hair and long legs, he seemed above it all, detached. His great friend was Dale Perkyn, the same age but much smaller in size, they went about with smudged fingers from the chemicals in his room, kept permanently locked against the rest of the house, and they croaked out 'I will ex-term-in-ate you' to each other and to all who crossed their paths.

When the family sat round the television at teatime, Shane insisted on the latest crop of space stories from the Promised Land, America. 'Don't the people over there have bodies?' enquired Philip sarcastically, as one talking head interchanged with another in succession. Shane only argued when playing cricket or chess and the younger children were given lets due to their age. He maintained the rules, and that they shouldn't be bent and it was up to the children to reach up to them. At the Wicca he supported his younger brother and sister against attempts to cut their sweets.

It was Hazel who decided on starting up the Wicca, after she'd taken a class from the Grammar round the museum in St. Edfric's, full of Saxon artefacts and militantly pro-Saxon in the way they were labelled.

The Wicca was held in Moon Farm sitting room on the first Sunday afternoon of the month. It was a family council where everybody brought up what was bothering them, and there was a vote at the end. Jandy attended as a non-voting member, going off into tucks of laughter when Lynnet tried to make drastic cuts in the children's sweets. 'We could make enormous savings if these children ate less sweets, *I* didn't get sweets. . .' she would point out.

'Lynnet you did have sweets. . .'

'Not like they do – sweets were still on points – remember? You've gone mad Mother, you're spending money like a drunken sailor. . .' – to a chorus of howls – and Lynnet's final throw – 'I promise to donate fifty pence from my Saturday wages to the holiday fund, for every pound you save if you cut their sweets.'

There was a snap election in the February. Harold Wilson wanted to increase the number of Labour seats in the House of Commons, the better to put through legislation.

Dr Barber hurriedly motored back from the continent in his big old Bentley to register his vote against. Hazel announced to howls from Lynnet and Jandy that she wasn't voting, she was sick of all politicians, and Alan martialled the Tory troops in Farthingale. On election day Lynnet was at school and Jandy was at Moon Farm. She tramped through snow in Lynnet's ponyskin boots and hooded coat to collect baby-food for Jasper at the village shop then take numbers at Farthingale primary which was the polling station.

Hazel and Rex were amused that Lynnet and Jandy believed in the idea of Progress, on their insistence that mankind was taking the upward path. Neither Rex nor Hazel had this view.

'Dare we attempt to re-enter the mystery of past cultures?" asked Rex in his quarterly magazine. "Dare we turn back to the spiritual wealth of lost civilisations? In the last two centuries we have seen the hasty discarding of our spiritual past, and now apathy, spiritual poverty and psychic disaster abound in this, our scientific age. . .'

'Something is always lost,' said Hazel, peeling circles of apple and letting them fall into pastry, for an apple pie. 'For every new advance, something is lost. . . It's so patronising, the way past ages are regarded now,' she said, 'as though they didn't know what they were talking about and understood nothing and were just ignorant fools because they couldn't flick a light switch. Nothing could be further from the truth. . . What are you smiling about?'

'I love the way you peel those apples – I want to peel them just like that,' said Jandy.

Hazel was one of the diminishing number of females who never wore trousers or a watch, it would go against her nature. Wearing trousers would make her feel confined, she said. When she returned to teaching she was obliged to clip a watch about her thin wrist. And on entering Moon Farm in the afternoons after school she would unclip it and drop it loosely, carelessly into a little dish on the hall table, because it was alien to her. She showed Jandy how to boil an egg without timing it. 'Just have confidence in your inner clock. Put the eggs in the pan and let it register in your mind and then you'll just *know* when they're ready,' she instructed.

'I just *know* when they're ready,' Jandy swanked airily to Margaret, who hovered unbelievingly over the egg pan and said tartly:

'Yes, well I hope you do. Alan won't want bullets for breakfast.'

Each morning when she opened the curtains of her bedroom Hazel looked across the fields to the Perkyns' thatched cottage. She imagined Jo, tucked up cosily inside with husband and child, as she herself had been with Rex and Lynnet when they first moved down into East Anglia.

'We loved it when we first came and I've never regretted coming here,' Hazel said to Jo. The Perkyns came from London. Paul Perkyn had been a policeman who hankered after his own smallholding, and Jo a former art student. She had taken floristry in order to get a job, but she hated it because it meant tearing up the flower heads and impaling them on wire to make horrid displays. The pair of them had worked with industry and pooled their savings and acquired a cottage with a few acres. Paul raised turkeys, vegetables and some corn; Jo grew vegetables and flowers to sell, as well as eggs from her hens. They had thrown themselves into life in

Farthingale with enthusiasm, had made friends with the Marlowes straightaway. Their son Dale went about with Shane. He was amazingly like the figure of St. Edfric, with chopped pale hair and stern unyielding expression. The parents were game for any fun or spirited activity going off.

Hazel listened to Jo's dreams and interpreted them, and after Jandy's lessons on poetry she heard her dreams too. She sat quietly, wearing a turquoise and pearl mandala suspended from a chain about her neck, twizzling it between fingers, touching it. It was like a chain of office, insignia of benign authority.

When she returned to Windy Ridge Margaret said briskly, 'Well I hope you're getting something out of this Jandy, I didn't know Hazel was qualified to analyse people, messing about in their so-called psyches or whatever it is.' Her diatribe left her bubbling with energy, she whizzed round the house with vacuum cleaner and mop.

More and more Margaret left all the pot-washing to Jandy. Her wedding ring was still provoking the red angry rash, which was greatly exacerbated when she put her hand in water. Rubber gloves were a must but she didn't like using them, so stashed up the dirty pots to await Jandy's arrival at midday.

'Jandy – Barny's on the telephone.'

'Oh. Right. Hello,' she said, coming in and speaking without enthusiasm into the receiver.

'Hello. There's a good film on in Thankful. Do you want to go?' asked Barny. He was a youth of few words.

'Okay,' she said ungraciously. It would be James Bond in a perishing cold village hall.

'You're very prejudiced in your own way,' accused Margaret. 'You hold it against Barny because he was at Gordonstoun.'

'No I don't. It's difficult for me to relate to him because he's not interested in anything much except the insides of cars.'

'Yes, poor Barny desperately wants to be a motor mechanic. I think that shows how serious he is – he takes the world seriously and wants to *do* something in it, to make a difference. . .' Margaret said warmly.

Barny's parents Major and Mrs Parr had bought Withy House from Hazel, and had camped out in the garden while waiting to move in. Thekla Parr had given Hazel a right talking-to. 'Look at the state you're in. That's what comes of letting a man walk all over you. Start as you mean to go on, and *never* let them get the upper hand.'

'That bloody woman,' Hazel had said, shuddering.

'And I don't think', continued Margaret, 'you're in any position to criticise Barny, because I don't see you doing any work.'

'I haven't criticised him, and Hazel has suggested I write down my dreams in a special book. . .'

'Oh has she – well I don't see how that's going to help you pass your exams,' Margaret replied truculently.

'You are supposed to be studying for your A-levels, not skivvying for Hazel,' put in Alan coldly.

'She's helping me with the lessons. And how come it doesn't count when I help Margaret in the kitchen?'

'That's not the point,'continued Margaret, 'you are here to take your exams. Alan has very generously said you could stay here.'

'Oh darling *really*,' protested Alan, 'I have been very fortunate, and if I can help Jandy in any way I'm pleased to do it.'

'I don't care darling, she's spending most of her time at Moon Farm doing nothing as far as I can see.'

'Well it's very kind of you to have me, and my marxist group said I could come.'

'Oh I see,' practically shrieked Margaret, 'I didn't realise you had to have their permission to come here.'

'I'm under a discipline Margaret, which is something you don't seem to know anything about.'

'Well if you're so very disciplined you want to get some work done – or you won't pass your wretched exams,' was Margaret's parthian shot, before taking off into the kitchen.

In spite of those fine words, Jandy felt undisciplined and worried about it. Her postal lessons arrived in thick brown envelopes at regular intervals, presupposing a routine. Each day she walked between the two houses, along the road that was a lane, past the gigantic horse-chestnut, clouds of green among the clouds of heaven, a line of Auden's ramming through her mind – 'to disintegrate in an instant in an explosion of mania/or lapse forever into a classic fatigue' – the dilemma of youth. She had begun to suspect the latter was her way, and in the face of society's problems it seemed the less worthy of the two options. Rex and Hazel had not been like this, they acted and had acted in the real world. They didn't hesitate.

In the afternoons at Windy Ridge the light came through the french windows and Margaret and Dr Barber sat puzzling over clues in the *Daily Telegraph* crossword. Reference books were consulted, words tried out. The pleasant afternoon sunshine played through the windows – was the heron on the pond? – get the binoculars – the air still, even the clouds in the wide sky seemed unmoving. Or they looked up his patients' symptoms in the big Mimms. When they broke off to complain about all the tea-breaks British workers had, or shake their heads over Mr Wilson, Jandy could have screamed. As the light came through the window on them there seemed an eternality about it that could never be broken.

Hazel and Margaret had a row over Lynnet and Paul Perkyn. Margaret accused her of not preventing their affair.

'You should protect Lynnet, she's only a schoolgirl.'

'Unlike you, I don't feel called upon to interfere in other people's lives, they have to work things out for themselves,' responded Hazel.

'She "doesn't feel called upon to interfere in other people's lives" ' mouthed Margaret to Alan. 'That's rich, coming from her.' She alluded to Hazel's amateur therapy sessions with Jo Perkyn, which took place twice a week in Hazel's sitting room, with her swinging the turquoise mandala, and getting Jo to talk.

'You've got it all wrong, she's still keen on Basil,' said Jandy definitely.

'That's all you know about it,' Margaret replied darkly.

Basil was the driver on the local bus, ever since Lynnet could remember, and when Rex left she had transferred her affections to him. Fatherly, moustachioed, he had mended her broken sandal, and when it went missing he stopped the bus and helped her look for her bike, which was not in the ditch where she threw it each morning, to be retrieved on the way home. Basil had been a driver when the Marlowes had just moved down from Manchester, and remembered the young mother and the toddler, asking questions on his bus about the new baby princess. 'But when did Philip put the seed into Elizabeth?' the child nagged. The passengers fell silent and sat with unreadable expressions, listening to the persistence of the child and the patience of the mother, who of course believed in answering every question, so they laboriously counted aloud back through nine months. 'Oh really Hazel – how like you,' Alan had said dismissively.

Each year Lynnet sent Basil a valentine. The food from her school cookery lesson was always short of a piece of pie or a bunch of cheese straws which he had sampled, and every summer she had another school photo of herself done for him. Some days, instead of getting off the bus on the Farthingale road, she rode back into Thankful with him, chatting.

'Lynnet has to do so much in that house, she's only young and it isn't fair,' said Margaret aggrievedly.

Next time when Jandy arrived back from Moon Farm at midday she found Margaret feeding washing into the wringer and in a filthy temper.

'I've had a visit from a man from the library,' she began. 'He called to collect your library book which is months overdue.'

'Oh,'

'Yes that's right – Oh. I couldn't find it so I had to give him five shillings Jandy, and you can just pay me back.'

Jandy went to her bedroom and fetched Sartre's *On Being and Nothingness*, which was one of the most boring books she'd ever read, but she would never have admitted it. She handed over the slim volume to Margaret, who read the title and exploded. 'Do you mean to say – West Suffolk County Council sent a man sixteen miles out in a car and I had to pay five shillings, all for a book about. . . NOTHING!' Her indignation built up to a high, peaked, and then she collapsed into laughter.

The sitting room at Windy Ridge was large and shadowed, in spite of the big windows. Chintz armchairs and sofas were lost in the big room. There were always flowers from the garden, or shaking hips in a brass jug in the autumn. Bird paintings hung on the walls, and Alan's father's paintings, mostly executed when he was a young man in Paris, before and after the Great War. Bookshelves on either side of the brick fireplace contained reference books and the Encyclopaedia Britannica, and the books from Alan's nineteen twenties' nursery. *Animal Heroes of the Great War*, *Wind in the Willows*, *Animal Husbandry*, and *Pig Farming – How to Survive It* stood next to a chunky collection of Pound's Pisan Cantos, forbidding and nebulously forbidden. Rex's books, autographed by him and with good wishes to newly married Alan and Margaret, had been removed after he decamped from Withy House and were now in the spare bedroom.

There were some of Margaret's favourite old books – the *Rubaiyat of Omar Khayyam* – a girlish passion of hers – and books about the Abbey girls, that Margaret lived in as a girl. The Abbey girls were soft and self-sustaining, there was an uncanny absence of parents, the girls organised everything by themselves. When Jandy was small and the parents went out Margaret would serve a fireside tea on a low round table, and tell of her doings as a schoolgirl, of the illicit Marmite brought to the school dining table in knickers, of the one sweet they were allowed a week – a Parkinson's Butterdrop – given to them on Fridays by Matron. 'The school had its own swimming-pool and its own library. . .'

'Gosh Margaret, how ripping,' six year old Jandy would

remark, having the lingo early, and delighting in the stories of the ivy-covered school and of the ghost that walked its corridors. As a child Jandy knew the world that surrounded them was not the world Margaret lived in.

In an old tin were snaps of Margaret at school, she and her schoolfriends in gymslips and black stockings. A photo of a dormitory showed a line of white counterpaned beds. It was the Rosebud Dormitory, where the small girls slept, and there was little Margaret in the second bed, holding a baby doll, a smile about her lips. When she married Margaret had cut off the words underneath the photo, but Jandy remembered them 'London Royal Orphan School & London Orphan School' – but she had left just the tops of the letters, so you could see where they had been. 'It was for orphans of the British Empire,' Margaret whispered proudly. She hated it to be called an orphanage.

When she had arrived in the summers to visit the newly married pair there were different things and overwhelming new smells of male and snuff. Alan had it sent from London in white packets with copper-plated writing. They lived at first in a golden-wood caravan, with cunning tiny cupboards and shelves and a darling little stove, and Jandy loved it when it rained as it was so cosy with the fire and bright continental striped blankets, and she collected all the farm cats and Rip the Alsatian together inside. Margaret and Alan's bedroom was pale blue and lavender, and smelt of the lavender from Grasse, for Alan had taken her there on the way back from their honeymoon, to stash up on the scent, bottles and bottles of lavender water and Number Five before it had the Chanel label on. And in the afternoons they took flasks of tea and sandwiches to the field where Alan and Tom were harvesting. Margaret waved and called against the distant whirring of the combine, which slowly clacketed to a halt, the field in a dream of sun and flying corn dust.

There was a dark unmentioned time when Jandy was small, and neither of them could do any right. If Margaret came back from dances late in the night the parents came shouting and accusing. When they had gone Margaret lay crying in the darkness. They never spoke of it but existed in it together, on a raft in a sea of hostility.

So when she bustled about in the caravan, pulling blankets from the cupboards at night-time and making thick sweet Horlicks, or when rain popped against the roof, Jandy thought of Margaret in her golden home happy, safe at last.

Margaret took her to see the favourite field, through a barred gate. On either side grew oaks and holm oaks, a wood way at the top, the ground covered in monster thistles with tiny fluffy heads, rampant and stretching overhead, the air dense with heat and fluff. 'This is where we've chosen to build. It's named Elijah's Pikle on the deeds. It was registered a hundred years ago by Elijah as his piece of land.' Margaret strode through the thistles in her tartan trews. There was a stillness, an enchantment on the field.

When their new home was built she came in the holidays and slept in the spare bedroom under an old blue denim quilt, a cider-press and boxes of apples in the corner, she was scarcely able to sleep for excitement and the scent of apples. In the cupboard hung Margaret's wedding dress – midnight lace – dyed now and worn at parties. And in the middle of the night, Margaret promised, if she left the window open, she would get a visit from Sabrina, the favourite cat.

Nobody could have been happier than Margaret and Alan when their baby arrived. Jandy visited beforehand and Margaret showed her the baby's room, bare except for Moses basket and a knitted pile of woollies. 'We must decorate, but it's hard to decide – blue or pink?' confided Margaret, eyes shining and happiness dripping off her like honey from a honeycomb.

'Orange and lemon,' said Jandy definitely.

When she next visited the new parents were locked fondly into worship, the baby in a sunny room papered with large orange and lemon sunflowers, his fiery little head in the midst.

The farm cats in the barns round the farmhouse had been gassed with the hens when Tony's broiler business collapsed. Those cats that split with Alan lived out their lives at Windy Ridge like a lost race, a living memory of the farm. In and out of the house in the day they hunted and mated in the Suffolk dark.

Jandy Lockhart to Andrew Quennell

Dear Andrew,

I hope all is okay with you. How is the Vietnam work? Down here revolutionary prospects are gloomy, they have no confidence in the good sense and fundamental honesty of the working class. It's sickening. Even Hazel doesn't like the unions. Lynnet is coming along, she supports the Vietnam work and we both go to the Labour Party meeting in Walsham every month – an awful trek in the cold unless Alan is going into St. Edfric's and can give us a lift. Last month we managed to get a resolution passed denouncing the ongoing attacks against the Vietnamese people and calling for the government to condemn the war. Margaret's wedding ring is giving her a terrible rash, which means I have to wash all the pots.

Love from Jandy

After she arrived back from Moon Farm she helped Margaret with the midday meal, Auden's poetry reeling around inside her head. In the afternoons, after a massive pot-wash, she took to her room to study. In the evenings, if Alan wasn't driving off to play squash with Barny or to amateur dramatics with Michael Turner, and so could give her a lift, she walked back to Moon Farm with the hurricane lantern, for a lesson and to stay overnight.

They discussed the poems in the set book – *Poetry of the 1930s* – Hazel alight over Dylan Thomas. Jandy saw it was what made her heart beat, and all her life never forgot Hazel reading out ' "The force that drives the green fuse through the flower/Drives my green heart. . ." ', with a kind of radiance under the brass lamps, the firelight darting light and shadow and Spotty snoring into the spilled ash in the hearth. Hazel was cool about Auden, whom Jandy liked best of all.

' "Man wants what he cannot have, not universal love, but to be loved alone" – that's so true, isn't it? Everything would be much better if humanity understood that's what the problem is. . .'

e

'What rot! Of course one wants to be loved alone. It's in the nature of human love, to be exclusive. You can't share everything.'

'Let's face it, Mother, it's time people understood they can't always have what they want and the world would be a better place if they loved everybody rather than one person,' said Lynnet.

'You aren't describing human beings as I know them,' protested Hazel, amazed, amused and exasperated all at once.

'No but Hazel the point is – who wants petty exclusive love, keeping out the rest of the world? I can't imagine anything more boring.'

'What a pair!' said Hazel to Rex.

The young Marlowes were showing off their new kittens to their Gran and Margaret and Mr Harker, who lived at the Hall and owned the Half Moon acres, all the way up to the horizon. He called at Moon Farm for the rent and a chat and a cup of tea, a rose in his lapel and old-world courtesy. He agreed the kittens were very fine, and Mrs Grove cried, 'Oh a tabby kitten! I love a tabby cat, we always had one at home, we had a lovely one before the War – the first war, I mean. Chilperry he was called. Now why was he called that? I've forgotten. . .'

'There was a musical show called Chilperic,' reminisced Mr Harker. 'The songs were everywhere. . .' Experimentally he hummed into the air, and the others watched while he tried to remember. 'I'm not sure how it goes, I saw it at the old Gaiety Theatre. . .'

Nick strode across the room and dumped the kitten in Margaret's lap. 'She's programmed to survive,' he said. 'Some cats are.'

The Marlowe children were quite practised at telling off adults. Alan had crossed swords with small Hebe on a number of occasions, 'What are you doing with that spade?' he interrogated her.

'I'm going to put a coat and hat on it. And what are *you* doing?' she had replied.

98

When Hazel started an anti-monarchy tirade, 'All this mimsying around in crowns and ermine. . .' and suddenly with glee, 'they do say he has someone else. Now who could it be?' Shane said sternly:

'That's quite enough Hazel – you sound like some awful gossiping old woman.'

And when Jandy for a laugh had addressed a letter to the Marlowe Coven, Moon Farm, she was roundly ticked off by Hebe when she appeared in the summer. 'Never do that again. There is a coven in the village and they might turn nasty if they think there's another one.'

'How on earth do you know that?' enquired Lynnet, amused and superior.

'We just do. We get to hear about these things, don't we, Nick?' Nick glared and nodded his head up and down.

Walking the lane to her lesson, past the massive chestnut tree 'sssssushshhing' in the dark, the hurricane lantern unneeded, the moon so bright. And another moon in the puddle at the end of the lane. She walked towards it, in it, and past, on her way to the warmth of Moon Farm.

Margaret and Jandy picked their way through the wood at the top of the garden, the dogs Rip and Judy crashing and wading through fallen twigs littering the floor, together with the tiny frail wood anemones. Big Kitten brought up the rear, stalking the party, periodically howling to be waited for, then darting ahead playfully. Breaking off branches, Margaret pointed out the young trees with their polythene guards that had been planted.

There didn't seem need of them, the wood was dense with foliage and undergrowth, the sky barely visible. They strolled through, and came out at the other side. The land here sloped downwards to the back of an empty cottage.

'Look – nut trees!' exclaimed Margaret, lingering in the cleared yard to see them. Then she went to peer through the low dusty windows, while Jandy broke into song.

'I had a little nut tree, nothing would it bear, but a silver

99

nutmeg, and a golden pear. . .'

'This would be perfect for you. I do wish you could live here,' said Margaret. 'It could be made so cosy, and you'd just be on the other side of the wood.'

'It's lovely as it is. But how could I live here? There's no work round here. . .'

'Yes but if you lived here you could find work.'

'But what would I do? It's miles away from anywhere. . .'

Through the window were flagged floors and a shallow ochre sink, its age marked in chips and discolouring. At the front of the house was a little bare lane with nothing in it except sky and hedgerow, and a slender mud road winding round into nowhere.

For Margaret and Jandy the house through the wood was part of a fantasy there had always been between them, that had coloured all of her childhood, and she recognised it for what it was – a fantasy that would never be a reality.

At Windy Ridge in those endless afternoons of crosswords and medical Mimms, there was one tantalising half-glimpse of another time. Margaret had been reading out the crossword clues and she let her attention wander through the newspaper.

'Oh really Daddy aren't people absurd sometimes – this article says that people on the bottom layer of society have more intense feelings than others. Don't they talk rot sometimes?'

Both Margaret and Jandy expected Dr Barber to agree it was rot, Jandy with the apprehension of bleak inevitability.

He said nothing, continued chewing his cake. 'I don't think that's at all true, do you?' chivvied Margaret.

He nodded rather than actually spoke, 'Yes,' his eyes closed briefly in agreement.

Jandy perked up and Margaret looked dumbfounded. 'You agree with what they say?'

He half-smiled, murmured, 'Yes,' his clipped manner making it quite clear the subject must not be ventured into further.

'It was rather a wild scene he and Alan's mother belonged to, I believe, on the Riviera just after the First World War,' Margaret said to Jandy later. His youth may have been wild but it was in some other place now and pushed out of sight.

At times when he was sitting waiting to eat, or in pauses between conversations, he played into the air gently with his finger, as though keeping time to melodies only he could hear. His fingers were held bent, not arthritically so, it seemed they were almost trying to catch some current or beam in the ether.

Every so often he would be seen across the field, tending a small bonfire, bursts of blue and turquoise, emerald and cerise flame, he stooping like a magician over his spells. 'Daddy's burning his old drugs,' Margaret said. 'It's the safest way to dispose of them.'

One time when he was on call he had a night-time dash through East Anglia – over twenty miles at three in the morning. He told them about it the next day with something like relish. 'It was a young couple and she'd fallen downstairs. It was quite obvious to me they'd been having a fight and he'd pushed her!'

'Oh dear.'

'Oh she was all right, I gave her some painkillers and he looked most contrite.'

When he wasn't on call he watched the horse-racing on television, and often backed horses, he had an account with Jon Warrender's book-makers, and took racing tips from Tom Feetham in the village, the pair of them exchanged racing anecdotes and were always pleased to see one another.

Tom lived with his mother and then, after she died, alone with his dog. He liked animals and followed the horses. He didn't seem to bother with women, he liked a sociable drink in the Half Moon but he wasn't a drinker, and Alan marvelled at how open and friendly yet impenetrable another person can be.

Margaret went off with Jasper to visit her parents for a fortnight and left Jandy in charge of the meals. 'I've explained to them you can only cook casseroles and flash-fry steaks, so they know. Now – don't forget – you must always do a pudding, and on the days when Daddy is locum you are absolutely not to let him dry the pots.'

Jandy nodded.

'And he's so good – please try to do his favourite at least once.'

'I'll see how I go,' she answered unpromisingly.

'We're having ordinary things,' she announced faintly defiantly to Dr Barber. 'Bread and butter pudding.'

'Oh, one of my favourites.'

She looked back at him suspiciously. 'And banana custard.'

'Wonderful.'

They got on pretty well. On Thursday afternoons he was late back for he went to drink china tea with a very elderly lady patient who had been a young woman when he was a boy.

On Fridays Farthingalers queued up at the fish and chip van which toured the villages, a weekly treat denied them on other days. Dr Barber arranged to collect the fish and chips and Jandy, freed from making a first course, attempted his favourite pudding – a proper chocolate mousse. It involved whipping egg whites in a bowl set into a pan of boiling water, and dropping in squares of chocolate. What a performance. Looking warily at the stuff it seemed okay, so she spooned it into glass dishes.

'Mmmmm. It isn't just the taste – I love the texture. They made lovely ones at the Café de Paris before the War. But this is very good,' he added hastily.

Bursting with success, she decided to try something else. There was an old waffle iron that Mrs Barber had brought from Belgium when she was alive, for waffles couldn't be obtained here. Jandy lugged it out of the recesses of the kitchen cupboard and looked at it for a long while, this contraption from another world, another time. Then she decided she couldn't cope with it.

On the last day of the week he came with some chocolate for her and a little oil painting he had done, of two flushed pears sitting in a dish of cream.

'I was in Paris at the beginning of the Great War,' he said. 'A fellow student and myself went out together for the last evening. We drank champagne, we visited one of the bals – not the Moulin Rouge, another one. There was an enchantment about Paris then and it's gone now. When the evening was over we shook hands, we both knew we would fight on opposite sides, and the next day he caught the train home to Berlin.'

'And after the War – did you make enquiries about him?' Jandy asked eagerly, wanting something like a happy ending. The barest of bitter smiles, the slightest of shakes of the head, and she saw the answer was No.

'My dear, civilisation is paper-thin. You have no idea. Young people now lead very protected lives.' He had lost an eye and a brother in that War, and wore a dark glass and a monocle; shrapnel still showed blue through the skin of his cheek.

Dr Barber had little to say about the Marlowes, and always referred to Hazel punctiliously as 'Mrs Marlowe', declining to use her christian name. When the Marlowe children descended en masse on Windy Ridge he beat a retreat, although he liked Hebe, whom he termed 'such a nice little girl.' He had been on call when she had gone down with mumps and so attended her and been taken by her conversation and her bedside books.

He and Mrs Grove too had warm conversations, for they were of an age and he respected her opinions although he didn't share any of them. She spoke high-mindedly of 'our role in society' and of poetry – she still used the Edwardian pronunciation which has passed away now – poietry.

'Oh she's quite a lady, and of course she's still doing sterling work. It's very necessary. But you have to be rather careful because birth control can easily slip into eugenics. And that's a different kettle of fish altogether.'

'I don't see why birth control should become eugenics,' declared Jandy.

'No you don't, but I've been around a long time, and these things have to be closely monitored. Once one boundary has gone, there's always another one to break.'

The mood at Moon Farm was suffused with excitement. Rex had arrived. He came in looking slightly thinner than last time but full of spirit. Handing a book to Shane, a bracelet to Lynnet, a doll and a car for Hebe and Nick, he nodded to everyone affably. He was here. Rex. He was among them. First he was taken upstairs by Shane to view the ongoing experiment in his bedroom, that no one else but Dale Perkyn was allowed to see. At first cursory glance Rex thought Dale must be one of his, he was always there to greet him in the sea of young faces. He had to look twice before handing the toy car to Nick. Then they went into the garden for tea and sandwiches.

'Daddy, look – my dolly, she has freckles,' cried Hebe, excited that he would be here, anxious for his attention. Hazel and Jandy came from the kitchen with fruit, to find Lynnet and Rex arguing: ' . . .you don't like anything that happens now,' Lynnet finished.

'You misunderstand me,' – he meant she wasn't being fair to him, but he would never have made that plea. 'I relish these 1960s, I'm delighted and energised by them. But what worries me is the amount of hope around, as though something difficult to face has been forgotten or deliberately buried. Humans will compromise their intelligence to sustain their hope.'

'But are we wrong then to hope?' asked the 18 year old girl uncertainly.

'It isn't a question of being wrong,' the man explained. 'It's likely we're all heading nowhere, that the only meaning in anything is what we give it. . .'

Lynnet declared roundly, 'Well I don't think we're going nowhere.'

Rex picked off grass from his old jacket, then he asked, 'If you were the Supreme Deity which feeling in you would be stronger – joy at the birth of a wonderful new life form that would immeasurably benefit mankind, or great grief at the death of a plague bacillus that would wipe out all trace of the human race in two hours?'

Hazel raised her eyebrows and looked amused, Philip laughed sardonically, Jandy looked gloomy. Alan, when posed the question later, said, 'Well I suppose Rex thinks he's very

104

clever, asking that.' Shane advised them to feed the question into a computer, only it must be a top one. Only Lynnet said immediately and adamantly:

'Joy at the birth of a new life form, of course,' and her confidence would often win the day and always see her through.

Reverend Radice, when asked the question at the Post Office by Lynnet, didn't seem troubled at all, he looked vague and waved a hand, as though waving the question away. 'Ah, the mystery of reality,' he said, and then tightened his bicycle clips and cycled off down the village street.

The Barbers had a party and a bunch of their married friends – Hazel, Michael and Madeleine, and the Warrenders – descended with their children.

Hazel and the Warrenders eyed each other, wary and polite. She suspected them of having encouraged Rex in the early days of his affair with Gillian. Jon Warrender and Rex were great friends, Jon would ring him frequently when they lived at Withy House, bursting with ideas for plots of new novels and excitedly intent on pouring them out. They were on the telephone for hours.

Pretty little Romaine Warrender, with dark eyes and retroussé nose, was curled up in an armchair like a cat, talking to Madeleine Turner and Hazel. They had all been pregnant together – Hebe, Sally Turner and Katy Warrender were all born in the same year, the husbands celebrated together each time at Hamlin House. Jon Warrender was a prosperous businessman, whose activities included ice-cream manufacture and insurance broking; he was a qualified psychoanalyst and took patients; he bought paintings and kept up with the arts. In addition, he was a leading light in the Easter Rabbits, an organisation of businessmen who put on shows and revues and did tap-dancing for charity. He managed to rope Alan and Michael into performing in their musical.

'Are you quite the right – er – build – to tap dance?' enquired Hazel.

'Well I will anyway,' said Michael exuberantly.

'So you're going to be a chorus-boy,' she said to Alan with glee.

'We'll come and hang round the stage door to get your autographs and pinch your bottoms,' Hazel and Jandy snickered away together.

Used to being ragged by lefty females, Alan closed his eyes very slowly and ignored them.

The summer was here again, Hazel and Nick went off to school without coats, Lynnet and Jandy swatted in their rooms for the exams, and at the Barbers throughout the day came the sound of:

   'whock whock whock

   "Oh I say Jack – Look at that!"

   "Yes Dan, he sure knows how to hit the ball."

   whock whock whock. . .'

At Moon Farm Sunday breakfast was laid out in the garden as brunch, the Perkyns always came and anybody else who dropped in.

After their exams were finished Lynnet and Jandy splashed candytuft paint on the sitting room walls, talking and arguing, their transistors on Wonderful Radio London, one of the illegal pirate radio stations. 'And now', said an excited voice tinnily, 'we're going over to Euston Station to hear Barbara, she's there with her guitar all day singing for passengers. . .'

'And another thing,' said Lynnet as she filled in a corner with paint, 'they aren't tackling the problems they said they would.'

'No,' agreed Jandy, 'they haven't nationalised the banks yet. . .' and at Euston Station on the half hour a little girl called Barbara swished her long hair and sang her song dedicated to the station, men in British Railways uniform brought her cups of railway tea, the white classical columns of the station were still in place. All over the country, all over the world, young people were making and singing songs about their lives.

Moon Farm garden was a mixture of old and new – the old buddleia, with its fluttering complement of red admirals; massive chestnuts at the side of the house; dusty priveted kitchen garden on the other side, with apple tree, where the family wash was hung to dry.

At the back, facing the kitchen window was a small rockery laid out by Shane and planted by him with dwarf marigolds and lobelia; and an orange rose, a free gift from a book club, rooted early one autumn by Hazel and Jandy when Hebe was unsteady on her legs and Nick still in nappies. Along the side were lilies from Jo Perkyn, under the high hedge which guarded the garden from the Half Moon acreage of fields, like the boundaries of a summer Eden. On the other side were pansies and sweet peas, planted for Margaret, who had called her baby Sweetpea in the Unmarried Mothers Home. "She's so sweet, she has a little wrinkled pink face, like a little flower, we call her Sweetpea, Mummie please let me bring her back," teenage Margaret had written and Jandy had read surreptitiously eight years later with a scowl.

'Did you ever think you couldn't go through with it?' Hazel asked.

'It never even crossed my mind – it didn't, in those days.'

'That's what I found alarming about pregnancy – the relentlessness of it, that this thing is going to be born and you just have to wait. . . Of course, Dr Coombes offered me an abortion when Rex left, although it was very late. . .'

Margaret was shocked, but thought Hazel was merely trying to keep up with current trends, pretending she had considered it. In reality it was the last thing she would have done.

The root of lilies from Jo were from her market garden, she grew flowers to sell in St. Edfric's – pinks and marguerites and stocks and sweet williams in massed ranks, cut off and put into tin buckets of water on market days.

Jandy was pleased to have something to do at Hazel's, because the plan for her to look after chicks hadn't materialised, the henhouses made so well by Margaret and Barny stayed empty.

Another plan was to have two calves to rear, now the farm was sold. But when it came to it, Margaret backtracked.

'Darling, I really don't think I can feed and tend two little creatures who are looking to me for protection, and then just suddenly turn on them.'

'Oh darling – really!' Alan said reproachfully. 'That's what people do, you know.'

'Yes, well, they do. I'm saying that I don't think I can do that.'

'Why, Joan Thompson-Bing. . . '

'Yes, Joan rears them for slaughter. I like Joan, I know all the arguments, and I eat beef. But I can't do it.'

Alan was aggrieved because they had cows for years when they had the farm, and he pointed this out. 'But that was a. . . a *herd*, darling.'

He roped in Thekla Parr, Jasper's godmother, to back him up.

'We don't have *any* nonsense like that,' Thekla said sternly. 'Pull yourself together.'

On her side Margaret recruited Hazel, who said at once, 'Heavens, no!'

Alan subsided, and the calves didn't come.

'Those calves aren't coming,' Jandy told Barny jubilantly, as they sat looking out at the rain over cups of coffee in Thetford's one cafe. Barny looked dumbfounded, slightly dazed, he blinked and peered ahead steadfastly, as though trying to see a path clear through this new way he was being picked on.

'How's Choppy?' she ventured. Choppy was Sabrina's brother, a handsome tabby. Barny made a non-commital but maybe slightly positive noise and nodded his head, which she took to mean Choppy was okay. When the rain stopped they sauntered through the narrow streets and stood before the new statue of Thomas Paine, a harsh gold, quill in hand like a weapon.

In spite of her complaints, Margaret also subjected herself to Hazel's scrutiny and advice. They spoke on the telephone every evening at ten o'clock.

One afternoon when she and Jandy were folding sheets and towels preparatory to feeding them into the ironer, Margaret said abruptly, 'Jandy I'm sorry your childhood was so awful.'

'Oh. Yeh.'

'They were so. . . difficult, Mother and Dad, so. . . lacking in understanding and. . . and. . .' the words trailed in the air. Jandy saw Hazel had advised her to speak of this subject that had never been mentioned.

'Hmmmm,' she replied cautiously.

'They were two miserable people without an ounce of charity between them,' Margaret burst out hotly, speaking of her mother and stepfather. 'And as for his political opinions. . . he's absolutely ruined you, that's what I mind.'

'He's more intelligent than you are,' Jandy replied rudely.

'Well thank you very much.' Then her indignation melted away and she started to laugh. Continuing with her remit from Hazel she said, 'When I had you I went to a Home near London – Croydon.'

'Did they treat you like naughty girls?' Jandy asked gaily.

'Not at all. They were lovely to us, nothing was too much trouble and there wasn't a word of reproach. They were true christian people – Methodists – and they couldn't have been nicer.' She smiled. 'There were all kinds of girls there,' she confided, folding a sheet and holding it pulled taut for the ironer to pick up. 'One super girl – Rosemary – she couldn't talk about it to her parents, because the father of her baby was an old friend of the family, a thoroughly respectable man, he had been their benefactor in some way, and it would have devastated them.'

'He sounds a lovely customer.'

'Well, yes. Her parents were expecting her back but she didn't intend returning home because she didn't want to see him. She had a little boy, but she left without him. She couldn't have coped on her own with a baby.'

'Why couldn't she?'

'Oh Jandy, it was so difficult in those days, you've no idea. . .' She took a sigh and then her voice turned lively again.

'Then there was Nona. She made us all laugh, she was the life and soul of the place, I couldn't imagine it without her. She was married and in her thirties, her husband was away in the War and she didn't want him to know she'd been having an affair. She was due to give the baby up before he came on leave but she changed her mind. "Oh blow old Staffy," – their surname was Stafford – "he'll have to put up with it, it's only one more and I'm keeping him" – she'd got so fond of her baby she took him back with her.'

'Who was Frances Mary?'

'How do you know about her?'

'There were pictures of a baby in that old tin of photos, with Frances Mary written across the corner.'

'She was Jean's baby. She still sent me photos long after I'd lost touch with the others. So she must have been very proud of her.'

This part of her life, so private, so perfectly remembered, made her smile, and she never spoke of it again, ever. Well perhaps she did to Hazel, who knows?

She vividly remembered the bedroom that the girls, strangers to one another, shared – the pretty flowered curtains, the pictures of Victorian heather moors, the text 'Come unto me all ye who labour and are heavy laden, and I will give you rest'. Talking at meal-times round the table; knitting over swelling stomachs; fire-drill. And pulling themselves from their beds at night, the sky full of noise, the imminence of a sudden hit and destruction, yet all of them illicitly carrying Life.

The next time he visited Rex was in high good humour. He had suddenly found himself involved in a lawsuit, and imparted the details to Hazel with relish.

An aged professor with an unusual name had read one of Rex's early novels and found the chief protagonist – Professor Gray Walta – had exactly the same name as himself, even to the idiosyncratic spelling. Rex read science mags for fun, and the name must have stuck in his subconscious. 'Apparently he discovered some connexion that was unknown in the brain. . .

110

And the best of it is,' chuckled Rex, not at all worried he might be horribly sued for every penny he had and hadn't got, 'one of the other characters is called Vivaine. She indulges in page after page of enthusiastic sex – and by sheer fluke the professor's wife's name is Vivien. There's no way I could have known that,' he finished up, 'but he's furious about it.'

Farthingale relished this scenario, Hazel was particularly gratified as Vivaine was based on her, as she pointed out to everybody. The Barbers and Turners felt quite warm towards Rex, and wanted to know the latest.

'I don't care. It will sell more books if he sues,' declared Rex, and went off to visit the elderly scientist to plead with him to reconsider. They got on well, he invited Rex to see his library and his laboratory, Rex was profuse with apologies and obviously understood a great deal of what the professor said. The name could stay as it was, said the professor – he was after all the personification of Wisdom – and Rex agreed to change the lady's name from Vivaine to Romaine, hoping Romaine Warrender wouldn't mind.

'Oh I say Rex, of course she won't mind. She'll be pleased,' Jon assured him over the telephone.

Farthingale was rather disappointed when nothing more came of the business.

The presence – or rather, absence – of Rex lay over all their lives in a sense. When the name Rex was uttered there was a catch in the air, a quickening, as though the invisible molecules all about were spinning faster. He wasn't there, but it was his territory, his name and his presence were layered into all their lives indissolubly.

'Look where the fairies have been,' laughed Jandy, at the rings in the lawn.

Hazel glared. 'Fairies – can't stand them.'

'Oh but I love fairies,' begged Jandy, as though pleading for existence.

'I don't love them. All through my childhood you got the

things – those blasted Tarrant creatures. The people who like them are frightened to look life in the face,' she asserted. 'It was the Victorians who started the sweetness and light and all the ickydoo that disguises what fairies really are. Fairies aren't benign, you know,' Hazel said severely. She was most militantly agin fairies.

'I still like them,' averred Jandy.

Acquainted with this exchange, Margaret laughed. 'Oh we believe in fairies here,' she said.

Jo earnestly told Hazel her latest dream, which she thought an important one. 'There was a chest with a harp and a shell on it, and when the music stopped playing the shell burst open and there was the most beautiful butterfly you've ever seen,' Jo said excitedly. 'What does it mean, Hazel?'

'Well now, if you think it's an important dream then you must trust yourself that it is. I think it means you have been seeking freedom for a long time and are ready to be free now,' Hazel said with an encouraging smile. They both sat smiling at one another. A message from the Unconscious. Could anything be more important?

Jandy implicitly believed Hazel's reading of dreams, and offered hers up, knowing she would understand her life better after Hazel had explained to her. But there was one dream she had had that she didn't report to the Oracle in its entirety. She dreamt she was in the service of the Black Queen Bee, she did the Black Queen's bidding and fought her battles. But she had stolen some eggs and held them carefully under her maid's apron, so as not to smash them. Not meeting the Black Queen's eyes she curtsied and dissembled.

In the garden Hazel and Jandy were talking and as they talked they watched the children – Shane and Dale Perkyn playing cricket on the lawn, Hebe and Nick letting a basket down from a bedroom window, with a collection of dolls and the tabby kitten in it. 'Be careful,' called Hazel, across the lawn, across the years. . .

'There is something utterly mysterious about what we do as

mothers. Something beyond personality. We fly very close to the sun,' she said quietly.

Their exams had finished, Jandy returned to Nottingham, and Lynnet got a job in the library at Cambridge, to start in September.

At the end of summer Hazel held a fancy dress party in aid of Oxfam. Paul Perkyn fixed fairylights in the trees, Hazel and Margaret cooked food and Jo made a huge open pie, cooked to her own recipe, of Moon Farm apples under a crust of cinnamon and sugar and hazelnuts from the Perkyns' trees. 'It's called an Old American Tart,' she informed everyone, with her big jolly hockey-sticks grin.

They all fussed with their costumes. Alan went as Sherlock Holmes, wearing the ulster that his mother, being continental, had had made for him because she had a romantic idea of Englishmen wearing them. Michael Turner swamped his cricketer's bulk in layers of dark cloth and went as a monk from St. Edfric's; Madeleine in a sari was an Eastern princess. Shane and Dale, armoured in cardboard, went as daleks, and were legitimately able to utter the stuttering noises they made a good deal of the time in any case. Hebe and Nick went as Alice and the White Rabbit. The best costume of the lot, they all agreed, was Jo's. She wore a black swimsuit and black tights and glittering antennae, with a spread of cloth attached to her wrists, which she had dyed herself in a rainbow spray of colours, and was the most beautiful butterfly any of them had seen.

Hazel, dressed as a gypsy, told fortunes in a booth made of sheets and as Michael took his place in the seat, he reflected on when he had first seen her – in Rex's shadow yet bloomingly pregnant with the child they lost. Now she swung her absurd earrings – another woman could have worn them, but Hazel's features were too small to accommodate them. 'Now,' she began, knowing what would go down well with him, 'I see a job promotion. . .'

'This is left over from when I was an extra on the film set

of Witchfinder General.' Paul, big and blond and bearded, told Margaret and Madeleine, indicating his leather singlet.

'Oh is it?' answered Margaret, agreeably enough yet in the slightly reproving governess tone she used with him. She was dressed as Flora Macdonald, with a swathe of plaid across her shoulders, and was expected to perform a sword dance later on, with Lynnet's schoolfriend Alison.

'What film Paul, why 'aven't we seen zis film?' demanded Madeleine.

'Oh it's been in the cinemas, I assure you. Vincent Price was in it.'

'I was a serving wench,' put in Jo.

Hebe and Nick were chasing round with the Turner daughters, got up as fairies, and two of the teachers from Hazel's school were helping Philip turn sausages. Sounds of laughter flew up into the trees and the wider circle of darkness, and soon a blue vapour rose and curled up from the barbecue.

Margaret was preparing for her dance with wooden swords brought by Alison, and Jill and Sally Turner nagged at their mother, who was now talking to Alan.

Alan found Madeleine appealing and relaxing, he could speak French with her and she was nothing like his mother, blonde and impossible, who was often demanding and made scenes in restaurants, making him cringe as a boy. 'Zis bloody country, full of bloody foreigners. . .' Thank goodness for his father, whose presence had smoothed away childhood cares, who smelled lightly of pipe tobacco and had an approachable authority. But his mother could be adorable, he was in awe of her, suddenly wonderfully sympathetic, she would at bedtimes tuck him in and say gently, soothingly, 'Dormez-vous et bien revée doux.'

Margaret tipped her head against the jollification round the barbecue thinking she heard Jasper, who had been put to bed in Nick's old cot. She excused herself, and hurried into the house. Up the familiar stairs, into the front bedroom, a slice of light from the landing enough for her to check Jasper without waking him. In the gloom she made out his brilliant hair damp across his brow, mouth open, clutched pudgy fingers which

114

she kissed and put under the covers, although it was so warm. On the high chest next to the cot sat the musical box, a fixture since the Marlowes moved in – a china boot with windows and doors and children hanging out of the windows. From afar she heard laughter.

It was Jo, laughing with Alan and one of the teachers, triumphant in her rainbow, noticing her husband was gone and light-hearted because she didn't care any more.

Lynnet left the garden and the shock of voices against the dark, hoping – knowing – he would follow. She turned into the way between the barns and when he came she surrendered to him and to the spinning lights, the distanced buzz of voices, the dazzle of rainbow, to everything her life was now and had been. All would change and she wanted this moment, to seal it into her life now, before it became the past.

Margaret Barber to Jandy Lockhart – *September*
My Dear Jandy,

It does seem ages since you left here. We hope your books arrived safely and they are the ones you require. How are you getting on at your classes? Have you found a job yet? Sorry to be so long writing, I don't know where the time goes to really. Although just lately I've been busy with blackberries, they have been magnificent this year. I have frozen about 4lbs and made 10lbs of jelly, which is popular here. Did I tell you Alan has a part in the next pantomime, written by Jon Warrender.

At nights Sabrina and Copperknob sleep curled up together in your gondola-basket in your room, all the rest sleep out. At the moment Teeny is romping with Big Kitten and Pywacket is asleep in the big armchair.

Hazel is going on to part-time teaching – she just cannot get anyone to do the housework, and had to turn down the post at Thankful which was hers if she wanted it. Rex was there last week, also Lynnet. Paul Perkyn is working for himself full-time now on the market garden – Jo does most of the gardening as Paul is putting up more greenhouses. Jasper is well and continuing to extend his vocabulary – he now says olly, for lorry. I have finished wallpapering, and it looks much better. God bless and write soon.

Fondest love,
Margaret

Rex Marlowe to Hazel Marlowe – *October*

HAZEL: You complain about the maintenance which I sent last month. I would remind you that you get considerably more from me than is taken home by a skilled worker, after overtime, who has to pay a mortgage and keep himself, his wife and family on it. If you can't do the same then I suggest you look to your own bad management.

REX

Hazel Marlowe to Jandy Lockhart – *November*

Dear Jandy,

Don't drop dead of shock on receiving this letter – feel flattered I'm devoting a free period to it! How is the studying going now or isn't it? Of course without my brilliant tutorials you are quite lost? I haven't managed to solve my domestic help problem, so now have Monday and Friday off. What is this 'ere new job you've landed yourself? Mrs Fielding sounds v. middle-clarse in her letter – quote: 'Her duty has been explained to the girl". I sent a reference explaining you certainly didn't need constant supervision. We had a smashing Hallowe'en party – we all got merry mainly on home-made plum wine – honest! It was vintage with quite a kick. Lynnet is having a Lynnet-type time in Cambridge. She has left her room – the old bird was too nosey and v. restrictive on her comings and goings. Jo is v. busy, she's making toys to sell on the market, all by hand.

There it is – the bell has gone and I must go and cast my pearls. . . Do write and let us have your news.

Love,
Hazel

Lynnet Marlowe to Jandy Lockhart – *April*

Dear Jandy,

I have moved again and am now sharing a flat with another girl, and upstairs are a bunch of nurses. We have a phone and a gorgeous little black cat thrown in, we also have a spare bed, if you'd like to come and stay. I have joined CND and the Chess Club. How are you? Still keeping body and soul together I hope. Still at the bookshop? Hazel said you were on the Easter march on the Monday, but I didn't see you. I suffered with blisters and how! I wore the shoes I did my canvassing for the General Election in – an obvious mistake. I got blisters after 4 miles and managed to stagger another 8 before collapsing into a first aid van. An unknown man saved my life by giving me a lift from Uxbridge to Waterloo. I stayed at Rex's on the Sunday. I had 8 large blisters, 4 on each foot, which had to be lanced twice. On the Monday, with about 3 yards of bandages, black socks and no shoes, I joined the march and quite happily finished it, and am looking forward to taking to the road again next year.

What is the Vietnam Solidarity Campaign? It sounds okay on the face of it – peace for Vietnam and an end to American aggression, and support for Vietnamese national liberation. That's okay. But certain people have told me that it's out for violence in Vietnam and communist domination. That I can't and won't support. Two undergrads from Caius want to start a Cambridge branch and want my support. Are they sincere in this do you suppose or is it a cover-up for something not quite so nice? Let me know what you think of all this. I suppose you heard Cambridge went Labour. The trouble is some of the city party are rather right-wing, and the Cambridge News is as Tory as Ted Heath. I've had a couple of fights with them already. When are you next coming down this way? Why don't we have a history weekend at my mum's? Thankful is still the sleepiest place on earth, I saw old Rev. Radish last time I was there, he was outside the Post Office talking to Dr Barber. Nothing seems to change, it's like a time-warp, and St. Edfric's as Tory as they come. I could write tons more, but the aforementioned undergrads are about to arrive so I must go and put the kettle on. Write back soon.

> Love,
> Lynnet

Postcard from Jandy Lockhart to Lynnet Marlowe – April

It's *great* if you're going to join the VSC. There's already violence in Vietnam so stop having qualms.

> Love from Jandy

PS will write a proper letter soon.

Hazel Marlowe to Rex Marlowe – *April*

Dear Rex,

The money was late again this month. If you aren't prepared to properly support the children you have fathered then I shall have to terminate Shane's visits to you.

> Hazel

Rex Marlowe to Hazel Marlowe – *April*

HAZEL: You should know better than to issue an ultimatum to me!

> REX

Margaret Barber to Jandy Lockhart – *May*

My Dear Jandy,

How are you keeping? We haven't heard for some time. On Sunday afternoon we went to Hebe's birthday party – it doesn't seem possible she is eight. Alan starts his new job next week, he has been trying to learn something about it before he begins. He is going to get a Triumph Herald two-tone green. It is a small car but quite nice and will be easy for me to learn on. Hazel is having Rex trouble, he has threatened to cut off her allowance if she doesn't let Shane visit. She is full-time now at Honington and has to cycle to the Duke of Marlborough each morning, where she is met and given a lift. She likes it but because of the transport problem is looking for a school closer to home. She wants to be independent of Rex. Have you heard from Lynnet recently? – if so you will have heard about Philip's leaving home without saying where he was going. Hazel's sister Ann is apparently frantic, she keeps ringing to see if he's turned up at Moon Farm. Alan has been helping to organise a village cricket team, there are some reasonable players in Thankful I understand. Teeny and Belinda are full of kittens, Barny has asked us to keep two for someone he knows at a garage. You should see the hedgerows here now, full of wild roses, and the roadsides afroth with creamy lace yarrow. I do love living here. Must away, Alan's father is taking me into St. Edfric's.

Fondest love,
Margaret

Hazel Marlowe to Jandy Lockhart – *June*
Dear Jandy,

How's life, and bookshops, and Andrew? I'm always open to hear a good dream! But when shall I hear them all – are you coming down this summer? Borrow Andrew's typewriter and put them all down – it will do you good to vocalise on paper. Did you hear about Philip? He was missing for a week, he turned up here one tea time, none the worse for wear, and just in time for flapjacks! Another wanderer – Spotty slipped his leash and what a dance he led us. Finally located at Thelnetham, Shane collected him – wet and filthy – he'd obviously jumped into a dirty old pond somewhere. Shane is now making him a pen with wooden posts and netting – quite a grand affair, it would house a family of lions. Hope to see you soon – there's a paintbrush at the ready!

> Love,
> Hazel + brood

Alan Barber to Jandy Lockhart – *June*

My dear Jandy,

The books did arrive! I thank you very much, they will provide me with bedtime reading for some time. You are supposed to be coming here but when? In other words will you let us know. We will send the money, so don't be proud. Work is going well, talking to people about insurance is much more in my line than selling cars – in fact, more than farming, and I am glad to have had this opportunity, thanks to Jon W. – altho' it is quite late in life to have decided what one can do best. Which is another way of saying – don't despair! Jasper is on top form and getting more conversant every day. I have been dipping into a magazine that was sent to you here, most of it devoted to a mad Cuban's speech to the sugar-cane cutters. Very red!

> Love from us all,
> Alan

Margaret Barber to Jandy Lockhart – *September*

My dear Jandy,

I am by myself as Alan is helping Michael get in his 'harvest home' – yesterday at 4.30, today from 5pm, after they both finish work. Michael has borrowed a combine harvester from a neighbour. Well the views of your 'happy band' are unusual, what a pity so many of them seem to be having marital difficulties. Marriage needs give and take on both sides, the ceremony alone just isn't enough, it takes work and commitment. But marriage – I can recommend it wholeheartedly! I am still pressing on with the driving lessons and go into St. Edfric's once a week with Madeleine.

We had a late visit to Dunwich, it was good weather

and Jasper loved the sand. Daddy fed the cats while we were away, he said they all cleared off after eating except Sabrina, she miaowed at him and seemed to want his company. The geese have got through the fence and made a mess of the garden – the geraniums are all tattered and seem to be their favourite flower. Must away and give Jasper his tea, so this must be all for now my dear.

Fondest love,
M.

Lynnet Marlowe to Jandy Lockhart – *November*
Dear Jandy,

I have moved again and can't remember who owes who a letter. Cambridge YCND is v. active now and beginning to stir up East Anglia. Recently a crowd of us went over to the USAF bases at Lakenheath and Mildenhall and swarmed over them – peacefully distributing CND leaflets. We were thrown out by the military police, but not before we'd managed to cover the whole base. Now Brandon YCND are going to attempt to march on Lakenheath, but I doubt if they'll get v. far. They won't have heard of our efforts because not a word was breathed about it in the press. But Cambridge CND's march at Alconbury was shown on tv. I didn't see you at Grosvenor Square on July 4th but knew you'd be there. Afterwards Dilys and myself went on to see the War Game at the International cinema in Bayswater Road. Rupert and Jonathan who were with us had literally gone as white as sheets. It was a marvellous film. What do you think of Harold then? I'm really cheesed off with him, he's made me more left-wing. Our own MP Robert Davies has been great – he's signed all the petitions over Vietnam. What are you doing now – still at the Bookshop? What did you think about Verwoerd's death? I don't condone assassination but if anybody deserved it he did. Now you owe me a LONG letter.

Love,
Lynnet

f

Margaret Barber to Jandy Lockhart – *December*

My Dear Jandy,

Thank you for the Christmas parcel. We look forward to opening it. How are things with you? Hazel is still working at Honington, Shane has started at the King Edward VI in St. Edfric's and Hebe and Nick are still at Thankful Juniors – there is talk it may close. Alan is absolutely against this and there may be some movement in the village to oppose it. Sabrina is well and lively, Big Kitten is beautiful and catches lots of things and always comes for walks. Jasper is getting very excited at the prospect of Santa's forthcoming visit. He watched me ice the Christmas cake yesterday. The baby doesn't take much milk but she seems well. Alan has a bad cold, he caught it I think at Hinderclay Conservative Christmas bash when he twisted all night and got too hot.

Fondest love,
Margaret

Hazel Marlowe to Jandy Lockhart – *December*

Dear Jandy,

Deck the halls with boughs of holly – tra-la-lala, la la la la etc – How are tricks? The moccasins are to wear while you stand on your toes to appreciate The Rainbow – hope you enjoy it – my favourite book. Built any more barricades lately? I tremble for the future and see dictatorships looming if this economic crisis can't be mastered and Marx is proved right yet again. Only it won't be dictatorships of the proletariat! The mad whirl to the great non-event (to use Rex's phrase) is in full throttle – crazy isn't it. I hope you have a Merry Xmas and I wish you were coming down.

Love from us all & the best to Andrew,
Hazel

Dr T. M. Barber to Signora Julia Ruggiero – *December*

Dear Sis,

A quick note to wish you Buon Natale, and to thank

you for your charming card. It was so good to see you all this year and I can only reflect how lucky we both are – the War, when we took different sides, way behind us now. The bambini here do very well. How good life is to us.

Teddy

Jasper Barber, dictated to Margaret Barber, to Santa Claus
Dear Santa,
Please can I have a football
a football game
some sweets
something for Victoria, she is very small
Love to you and all the reindeer,
Jasper XX

Margaret Barber to Jandy Lockhart – *December*
My Dear Jandy,
If you need to change the skirt, let me know. Many thanks for your presents – Alan has worn the tie (and he can be funny about ties, so he must like it) and Jasper likes his lion. He is full of beans, he plays his guitar and fires his new gun every day – Shane gave him a good one with caps. Rev. Radice called round today for a sherry, and to arrange a time for Victoria's christening, in February. I hope she will not cry. He supports the village school staying open and will sign the petition. Hazel, Jo & Paul are coming to see the New Year in with us. Jo has been quite ill with a blood complaint and has to take things easily. I have been doing the Perkyns' washing for three weeks. I gather from Hazel that she (Jo) is in a funny frame of mind about things in general and Paul particularly. Hazel says Lynnet is head over heels with an undergrad from Downing. We all wish you a very happy and peaceful New Year.
With our love,
Margaret & Alan

4

CONFLICT

The next spring Jo Perkyn ran off with their temporary lodger, Billy, who was there studying Agricultural Economics. Hazel was aghast, and when Jo called to say goodbye tried to dissuade her from leaving.

'No – I've never felt so right about anything. You've made me see that freedom is essential, that marriage is a prison. . .'

'But what about Dale? . . . and. . . and your flowers?' asked Hazel in desperation.

'My mind is made up. I've never felt more sure,' replied Jo.

Hazel's therapy sessions had born fruit; she would miss Jo. Paul and Dale stayed together in the cottage. The Barbers blamed Hazel.

That summer Hazel decided they would move, the entire family, to Lyme Regis. 'It will be a new start. And I shan't have to pick up any more pieces after other people,' she said, balefully eyeing Jo's postcard from Wales on the mantel.

She was still smarting from the telling off Alan had administered: 'Well Hazel, I hope you are thoroughly ashamed of yourself.'

'I'm tired of incompetent folk dumping their problems on me,' Hazel said fiercely. 'Not just Jo – those two – Margaret and Alan.'

Hazel took Shane to see the new house and sight-see round

Lyme, and Jandy came to look after the small children, she cooked them bubble and squeak for breakfast and let them wear whatever clothes they wanted.

Late at night Mr Petch's taxi drew up outside the front gate. Hazel and Shane were back, tired out from their day. The children were in their nightclothes, ready for bed, but Jandy had allowed them to stay up to see the wanderers, and they started clapping when the two of them came in.

'We'll have cocoa, and then we must all go to bed,' said Hazel. 'Lyme is wonderful,' she added dreamily. They had wandered round, Shane had eaten as many ice-creams as he wanted and was photographed with a parrot on his arm by a street photographer. 'The house is ideal, you'll all love it, and Lyme too – we walked around and we saw the cliff where Louisa fell down in *Persuasion*, didn't we, Shane?'

'Did we?' said Shane good-naturedly.

'Mummy, do you think somewhere there is another planet where other human beings live?'

'Oh bound to be, dear,' laughed Hazel. Behind his sober expression small Nick was thinking of the Other Children, four of them like the four at Moon Farm, and Rex and a different mother.

They went happily to bed, making plans. Hazel made enquiries about the schools, a contract came to be signed for the house. But arrangements fell through, hearts became faint, and it proved a mere dallying between the interstices of the big love affair that was Moon Farm.

Their world was a strong world, a resolution in itself for the ills, slights, hurts of the wider world, there for the people who were maintaining it. For all their differences, the Barbers and the Marlowes were part of each others' lives both imaginatively – they relied on the others' good opinion – and practically – Alan took Margaret and Hazel into St. Edfric's each week to collect groceries. Jasper Barber could be seen playing in the striped Ladybird top that had been handed on from Nick; baby Victoria's best dress was a little smocked frock sent from Manchester by Mrs Grove. At parties Hazel turned up looking sparkle-eyed in the sapphire velvet evening suit abandoned by Margaret. In Nottingham Jandy wore a green silk crossover top that had hung in Hazel's wardrobe since the 1940s. She put brilliant blue bugle beads with it and went off to a July 26th party. Each May Hazel treated Margaret and Alan to tickets for a concert at Lavenham church, to hear Yehudi Menuhin – one of the passions of her youth. The three of them took their seats in the dark church, overflowing with people and expectation.

Lynnet threw herself into her new life in Cambridge, joined CND and the Chess Club, and each time she wrote to Jandy it was from a new address.

With great enthusiasm Margaret stitched her a ballgown for the May Ball, Lynnet came home at weekends to have fittings, and when all was ready, each flounce and tuck in place, bought her an evening bag to match. 'She looked so nice – so young and fresh and determined to *enjoy* herself,' approved Margaret. Hazel stayed amused and detached, Jandy wasn't there, but when she visited in the summer called the enterprise bourgeois escapism.

'Yes dear,' laughed Hazel.

'Oh you would say that, you disapprove of everything we do. I just wished I was doing it for you,' said Margaret sadly.

'Honestly Lynnet, the students in Paris are tearing up the pavements with their bare hands to dismantle the system and you're togging up to join it,' Jandy admonished Lynnet, who grinned.

'I don't remember Paris being like that,' said Dr Barber. 'Everything has got out of hand nowadays.'

At Windy Ridge Alan fixed a swing for Jasper, thick ropes hanging from the limb of a great oak tree. 'Oh it's delightful,' murmured Hazel. 'Utterly delightful.' Looking round the garden at the rockery, with birdbath and cosmos; at the pink fountain of roses under which lay Judy the little black spaniel, with one of her puppies, Spotty's brother; at the hedgerow and

126

great waving trees, and the vista across the fields to where Dr Barber lived. She saw Margaret making coffee in the kitchen, and Jandy collect the washing from the line, going along and feeling each garment, detaching the scallops of baby Victoria's white petticoat that had got caught on the pink knots of incipient fruit in a young apple tree.

Inside the house Margaret and Hazel sipped their coffee, Jandy set up the ironing board and fetched in the basket full of dry washing, then played a singing pat-a-cake with Victoria:

"Some talk of Alexander
And some of Hercules
Of Hector and Lysander
And such great names as these. . ."

. . .just as teenage Margaret had played with her, whilst the voice of David Attenborough beebled away in the background, '. . .the young females not yet mated are looking after their mother's young. . .', and the new Great Dane puppy tugged at the covers of an armchair.

'I know a joke,' offered Jasper.

'Go on then.'

'There was a lady with a parrot and she was waiting for a bus, but when it came it had a notice up saying No Parrots Allowed On This Bus – stop it. *Stop* it.' He ran to his mother complaining, 'She's laughing and I've not told my joke. Mummy tell her to stop it.'

'This one is going to be true-blue,' said Margaret proudly, watching Victoria clambering about on the floor and determined to get things right this time and not be landed with a changeling.

'I don't see how you can tell that, she's only a baby. Unless you brainwash her, of course.'

'You can talk. What have you been teaching Hebe and Nick?'

The Barbers' pretty little bantams picked about in the garden. Margaret had heard that bantam eggs although small were good for children because they were particularly nutritious. Goodness knows why Margaret and Alan were so against Rex's plans to incorporate two females into one

127

household, for they followed the doings of the bantams with approval. Cocky, in his smart lacey cavalier collar, went strutting about the garden accompanied by his two little wives, and when night fell the little creatures roosted up in the trees together.

At Moon Farm the curtains were drawn back on another day. 'Wake up folks – the world doesn't change for the better – yet again the human race has disgraced itself,' announced Hazel, throwing open bedroom doors one after the other. 'Russian tanks have gone into Prague. . .' There was a howl from the beds, prostrate sheeted forms turned and groaned.

'What did I tell you? Human nature doesn't change,' remarked Alan calling by later that day.

'Oh people say that, meaning it's not worthwhile making the effort,' batted back Hazel.

'Oh God, every time I come here I have to listen to a lot of left-wingers moaning and dripping and wringing their hands,' remarked Philip to no one in particular.

What a year. Martin Luther King had been assassinated and then Bobby Kennedy. In late August the television screen was full of anti-war protesters at the Chicago Democratic convention, in turmoil with Mayor Daley's police force. But when Dr Spock was convicted of abetting his now grown up babies to avoid the army draft for Vietnam, Moon Farm and Windy Ridge were in shock.

Nothing rocked Farthingale like the Great Dummy Row, when Victoria was a baby. Tempers became short and scorn was tossed into the air in the general direction of the other camp. Jasper had been a fat, red-haired sunny baby, but Victoria was tiny and wouldn't eat and howled much of the time and wouldn't be comforted. Alan consulted his father. His unceremonious workaday advice was, 'Give her a dummy. They are much maligned things, used with discretion they do no harm.'

Dr Spock – regarded as a bible by both Hazel and Margaret – had the same advice. But in this one instance Hazel was disdainful, as though she came of a breed separate and superior to the ordinary human race.

'Dirty, unhygienic, filthy things,' she began. 'They encourage quiescent babies, there's nothing worse than seeing a lazy mother shove a dummy into a pasty-faced bawling child,' she railed.

Margaret, insulted that by implication her infant was being called pasty-faced and bawling, replied energetically. 'Well I think what you did to Shane was dreadful,' She turned to Madeleine. 'He cried a very great deal as a baby, and Rex and Hazel used to push his pram into the next field, because they couldn't stand to hear him screaming, and they wouldn't give him a dummy, it was against their precious principles.'

'Oh Margaret, no – 'ow cruel,' and she burst out laughing.

Jasper Barber to Jandy Lockhart
Dear Aunty Jandy,

It is a free period. I have done my prep and we have to write letters now and I am writing to you. It is my birthday soon and mummy will be making my cake I want a game called Striker for my birthday it is brilliant. Last week we went to Bressingham gardens I went on a train and I had a nice cream. I hope you are all right.

Love from Jasper.
PS my birthday is next Thursday.

Hazel finished school, walked the two miles from Farthingale, fed Spot and made sure Hebe and Nick were washed and tidy, before walking with them to Windy Ridge for Jasper's birthday party. She left the children to play in the garden, rang the doorbell and walked in. Margaret sat rigid in a chair, staring into space. In the kitchen were piles of dirty pots and pans from breakfast.

'I can't go on,' said Margaret, not attempting to move.

'Well forty children will be coming in half an hour, so you'd better get a move on Margaret. I'll wash these pots while you lay the table,' instructed Hazel firmly, pushing her towards the table and quashing the fury that was rising inside her, after she had done a day's work. 'And then you put the strawberries in the dishes while I make the jelly.'

'I don't know how she managed to get so many pans dirty while cooking a simple meal like breakfast,' she told Lynnet afterwards.

It was 1969 and everyone was calling it the Summer of Love.

In Farthingale it was also the chive summer, for suddenly the inhabitants were growing it in their gardens and scattering it far and wide in salads and sandwiches and scrambled eggs – wherever they could put it they did. Windy Ridge was bursting with children, cousins visiting in the school holidays, they played table tennis and climbed trees, and Margaret ran round refereeing games and quarrels and putting Smarties in plastic beakers for Victoria and her cousin William. At Moon Farm Lynnet and Jandy turned up with their boyfriends in tow, the old record-player sang out 'Je t'aime, Je t'aime,' endlessly, they played cricket in their swimsuits and at the end Hazel turned the hose on the lot of them. Hot day led into hot day, they discussed vegetarianism, and what constituted the ideal society, and what would you really do if you could press a button and save a million people but kill yourself, or save yourself and let them all perish.

Dashing about with paintbrushes and arguing at the same time, they painted the children's rooms cream and the bathroom startling pink, and afterwards Lynnet took the brush and painted a big heart outside the back door, with Make Love not War lettered inside it. Nobody's initials, Hazel noted – a heart signifying universal not personal love. 'Man wants what he cannot have, not universal love but to be loved alone,' echoed back to her from the year when the girls were taking their A-levels.

They only painted the woodwork downstairs that summer, Hazel had forestalled them by hanging a ludicrous paper on the sitting room walls, patterned all over with a little man serenading a flowered senorita on a balcony. Everybody entering the room groaned, especially those who fancied themselves halfway sophisticated, but Hazel said, 'I don't care, it makes me laugh,' and it *was* impossible to view without bursting into an involuntary grin. Matching the splash of flowers in the senorita's hair and the scarlet sash of the strumming little man, outside the tomatoes ripened under the windows, the plants getting taller and taller, their red globes peering in.

Hazel was having problems with Rex. He accused her of being too demanding. She put the telephone down on him and refused to make the first move. Rex seemed to be developing an ongoing paranoia about powerful or would-be powerful females. When Germaine Greer announced she no longer wore knickers, a fuming Rex wrote a letter to *The Times* about it. Merriment percolated between Lynnet and Jandy, but no words could describe the scorn in Hazel's expression. His next book came out and was called *Men – the End of the Road*, in which the last few remnants of the male population were hunted down by prowling armed females. It sold well and was printed with a flattering quote from Arthur C. Clarke which belonged to another of Rex's books dealing with intergalactic travel and was nothing to do with female underwear or sexual warfare.

Then they landed on the moon and Shane and Dale went round chanting, 'Neil Armstrong, Buzz Aldrin, John Glenn. . . *ye-e-e-es!*' lifting their arms in enthusiasm, cracking the astronauts' names into the summer air. Shane went off to visit Rex, and the two of them gloried and celebrated together over the moon-landing.

Shane regularly went to see his father and enjoyed his visits. Hebe and Nick were judged by Hazel to suffer after-effects from Rex's company, they didn't visit and watched their elder brother go off with relief and slight annoyance.

'Let's go back the Thelnetham way, I want to show you something.'

'I hope this is worthwhile Jandy, I have things to do,' said Margaret, detouring down the lanes and stopping the car outside the old churchyard.

Jandy got out and went over to an ivy-clad holm oak, near the place where Hazel and Rex's dead baby lay. 'See,' – she waved a paper. 'Hebe posts letters to the Fairy Queen through a hole in the tree.'

Your Majesty,
    I entreat you to look kindly on the family at Moon Farm. Please look after our baby brother we never saw, help Shane with his experiments, and don't let Spotty get lost when he runs away.
                    Your subject,
                    Hebe

Margaret was much amused. 'You'd better put it back or Her Majesty won't get it,' she said, starting the car.

The young Marlowes called their hens after the wives and daughters of Henry VIII, with the change by consensus round the breakfast table of Bloody Mary to Broody Mary. Hebe would come in from the barn and announce 'Elizabeth the First's laid her fifth egg this week', or 'Katherine of Aragon is off her lay.'

'And where', demanded Rex, on a visit, 'is Henry?' His paranoia painted in the naked male bird on a dish, two imploring feet tied together in the air.

'Oh we don't have a Henry – he's not necessary – we manage without,' said Hazel triumphantly, giving him her special Bette Davis challenging look.

After the family holiday that summer they returned with a kitchen picture of a smirking hen announcing, 'The cock does all the crowing, but the hen lays the egg'.

'It's terrible Hazel, it's female chauvinism,' criticised Jandy.

'Yes dear,' laughed Hazel buoyantly.

Rex rang suddenly and demanded to take the children out. Hazel agreed, and Shane, Hebe and Nick went off to the seaside for the day, coming back as promised for eight o'clock. 'Then' related Hazel to the Barbers, 'he sat them down and proceeded to inform them that his doctor said he had a bad heart, he wouldn't live another ten years, he might die at any minute. They didn't know what to say. Shane of course is never fazed by anything, he's used to Rex, he said he was sorry, but the other two looked scared to death. I practically kicked him out and we had a thumping row on the phone the next day. He's not taking them out again in a hurry.'

Burning with resentment at the indifference of his children to his mortality, Rex drove away from Moon Farm and in the opposite direction to his home. He drove until he hadn't the faintest idea where he was, until the petrol indicator waved dangerously low, then he got out and slammed the door, neglecting to lock it. He took a swift gulp of the brandy kept in his pocket, and made his way forward. He appeared to be at the edge of moorland, and in the distance he saw a spark moving rapidly, liquidly against the dark, shivering orange and yellow, smoke speeding upwards – a fire. Round it he made out huddled forms, hands held forth the only solid thing visible, and he felt a sudden urge to seek out the company of those who would be abroad on such a night.

As he neared the fire one of the forms hailed him.

'Ah-ha,' it said fiercely, regarding Rex with what he could see now was a baleful eye. Then he was silent.

'It's the Cloutie,' offered another of the company. 'Dinna gie him onything ta drink.'

'He's nae the Cloutie,' said another scornfully. 'But he's frae the Cloutie.'

Rex didn't enquire why folk with Caledonian accents would be so far south, but said, 'Friends, I don't need any of your drink,' and he brought out the bottle from his coat.

The eyes round the fire sharpened, he seemed to notice. One of them held aloof at the brandy, and he instinctively felt warm towards him. But when he offered the man the bottle, he shook his head. 'His wife's left him,' explained another, non-Scots voice.

'Congratulations,' said Rex heartily, clapping him on the shoulder. 'I wish my wives would leave me. Wives are an infernal blight on decent folks' lives. If I were to tell you,' he began, and thought better of it. In fact, he couldn't remember what he was going to complain about, just an immense sense of being wronged by the women he had cared for over the years surged over him and left him dumb.

'It's not bad,' he said, at the sip of their bottle, thinking it the worst stuff he had ever tasted in his life. But after a while it changed its nature, became something that was part of this world and that he ceased to find remarkable. His mind had become benignly numb, his faculties in limbo.

'Look!' he said then suddenly, pointing to the fire. 'It's Hazel.' The company followed the direction of his finger, to the flames leaping about and licking at the night. 'Hazel. She's taken everything. Everything. She bleeds me dry. . . As soon as I started to succeed – you know' – he addressed the man on his right in a wrecked tweed coat, 'how important it is for a man to succeed – just at one thing – just – one little – thing' – he could scarcely get the words out. 'She resented it. She resented it. She – pulled the rug. . . from under me. The rug. The rug,' he reiterated. It was important. 'And there's Gillian. She's different. But she wants her own way. . .'

They all nodded. 'Ah.'

'They take everything you've got, everything you are. The wives. The children – they don't care about my bad heart. I'm a provider. That's what I am.' There was definite movement of sympathy in his direction now, he was speaking a language they understood.

'Women's Lib,' he just managed to bring out the hated words. 'Let's drink to it. Let's drink to the wretched witches' brew. . . they call Women's Lib. . . what a poisonous potion. . . Still each age has its trials. . .' Even hopelessly drunk Rex took the long view. As he collapsed near the fire they pulled him out of its way, took his bottle and most of his money, leaving a few coins for a telephone call. The man who had refused Rex's drink made a pillow for him with a smelly old cardigan and tenderly pulled his jacket across.

He woke with an immediate sense of grievance, before he'd even remembered who he was or how he got there. His neck was stiff and aching, his legs cold. Still. He lay almost without moving, not wanting to resume his life, wanting not to remember anything. The sky was slightly lightening and way into the ether a pale star lingered in the morning dusk. Rex lay on his back and watched it. Lifetimes of years away, it probably no longer existed, we were seeing a phantom. His mother. She would be the only person to care about his failing heart. But he hadn't been home for a long time. His parents were both placid God-fearing folk who paid the world its due and kept a grocery shop in a north Derbyshire village. 'Manchester Grammar' his form teacher had said, the word sparking and igniting into his life. It was one of the best schools. 'You could get to Manchester Grammar, Marlowe.' Even in the juniors they called the boys by their surnames, to make them tough. 'Manchester Grammar' he repeated to his mother as she insisted on tying his woollen scarf round his neck and pushed a packet of sandwiches into his pocket. She had looked back at him, her lips primmed up, cautious, half-frightened, but wanting to believe.

The juniors was a little grey Victorian school, with old-fashioned teachers, old-fashioned lessons. Fractions. Clauses. Decent handwriting. Bible stories – even the art lesson was painting bible stories, Moses in the basket and Noah's Ark with a rainbow and Elijah coming out of the clouds in a chariot. Poetry. That's what had moved him. The short poems in old wrecked books with the pages missing. That first time he had felt something different – he had walked home through the village streets his head bursting with elation. 'We who with songs beguile your pilgrimage/And say that Beauty lives though lilies die. . .' How did it go? 'Death has no repose/Warmer and deeper than that Orient sand/Which hides the beauty and bright faith of those/Who made the Golden Journey to Samarkand. . .' Yes, yes – he still felt the excitement.

'When those long caravans that cross the plain/With dauntless feet and sound of silver bells/Put forth no more for glory or for gain/Take no more solace from the palm-girt wells./When the great markets by the sea shut fast/All that long Sunday that goes on and on/When even lovers find their peace at last/And Earth is but a star that once had shone.'

The world was suddenly a different place, he had shaken and nearly burst with emotion at the possibilities, the unknown tragedies that beckoned him forward. His village, his whole world a tiny speck of dust in a turning endless cosmos. Rex got up from the cold ground, shook himself and cursed and found his car-keys. The pale star was fading into the morning, soon it would be gone. The voice of his doctor took over in his mind, and in order to forget it, he hurried to find his car and go home to Gillian.

In her bed faraway Jandy sighed in her sleep and dreamt of Moon Farm in the winter, the land covered in a white and silver crust, the air icy, snowflakes like possibilities whirling around her head as she walked. She opened Moon Farm gate and the trees of summer waited for her, the air balmy with flowers and eternal blossoms.

Hazel Marlowe to Jandy Lockhart
Dear Jandy,

Happy birthday! What's new pussycat? How many more barricades have you built? Lynnet's wedding went off very well, but she was so nervous poor girl that she trembled from head to toe. Alan and Margaret were *most* affable to Rex, who faced it out in the end. All relations had a good time, so at least they were happy. *What* is happening in the old USA? And here, Vietnam government dossiers going missing. . . Could it be a split in the establishment, so that one half of same can lead the revolution and survive? Philip announced when contemplating the hens that he had discovered nirvana – he wants to be a hen. If he achieves it he will be truly blessed to escape so from this mad bad world that can also produce the likes of Menuhin. Just been to another of his concerts – oh boy: Margaret and Alan are going to Dunwich in early August, and we'll be back from there on the 9th, so do stay over.

Love from Hazel and company.

A month after the wedding Margaret sent for Jandy, to spend time with them before they went on holiday, to make tea for builders doing alterations in the house, feed the animals and the Marlowes' hens whilst they were away, and stay over with them when they got back.

Alan met her from the station, took her case and loaded it into the car, and started up the engine. 'Do you know what they're doing at Moon Farm now?' he demanded abruptly. 'All those children are calling Hazel Hazel.'

'Well that's her name!'

'Of course it is,' he burst back exasperatedly.

'I don't catch your drift,' she said, catching his drift exactly but making him spell it out.

'Well if you can't see anything wrong with it I feel sorry for you. It shows utter lack of respect, it encourages them to be forward. . .'

She leaned back and watched the Suffolk lanes go by, in the wind the wheat moving and flickering like diamonds, as he talked on.

Margaret and Alan and children went off to Dunwich, and left Jandy in the house with the roof off and the tarpaulin flapping. When she went to Moon Farm to feed the hens she brought Spot back with her for company and in case of burglars. At nights she barracked herself into the bedroom and put a chest of drawers in front of the door, reinforced on top with Victoria's dolls' house, and settled Spot on a blanket in the corner. At every noise, every squeak, and each time the tarpaulin rose creaking in the gusts of wind, Spotty howled dismally. He finally crawled to the bed and went underneath whimpering.

In the daytimes she made tea for the houseful of plumbers and roofers and plasterers, then went for long walks in the empty lanes. The Marlowes should be back about now, she thought, but it would probably be tomorrow before she would see them.

As darkness flooded over the flat land very suddenly, she dreaded another noisy night, and fell upon the telephone when it rang. It was Hazel. 'We're back. Are you coming?'

'I'll come now,' she sang back joyfully, going at once to leash Spotty and lock up and light the hurricane lantern.

There was no need for it, the moon was as bright as ever it could be, a moon that you couldn't believe – monstrous, round; gold and swollen, humping up at the end of the lane. A moon such as you never see in town, because buildings hide it – a golden moon, a moon out of an old tale, unbelievable, as though it would take over the earth itself, as though you could touch it when you reached the end of the lane.

'Look Spotty.' Spot danced about and tugged on his rope, excited to be going home and away from the empty creaking house. She put out the unneeded lantern and they walked along in the summer night towards the looming golden globe.

She waved to Dr Barber and Mrs Kettle, his friend, and they came to speak to her through the open kitchen window. Mrs Kettle, who had been a model when young, looked quizzically at her combat jacket, but Jandy didn't care because soon she would be at Hazel's. Spot tugged, anxious to be on the way.

'Whatever is she wearing?' asked Mrs Kettle.

'Oh she's one of the troops,' answered Dr Barber drily, taking a wet plate from her hands and wiping it. They finished their chores, and then went through into the sitting room. Mrs Kettle seated herself at the piano and let her fingers stray over the keys and then began playing the popular tunes of Dr Barber's youth. 'You are my heart's delight and where you are I want to be. . .'

Jandy and Spot were back in the path of the moon, on the final leg home.

'Hello dear – come in.' Hazel at the front door, almost tiny in the light that suddenly flooded from the house. And in they went. Hebe was in the kitchen making a meal, Shane and Nick were mending a bike. Spotty was delirious with joy, he turned about several times chasing his tail, then shot upstairs.

Jandy settled herself down on the old plum velvet sofa, in the pools of light from the lamps, in her very favourite place again at last. Her eye took in the well-known objects – the silver samovar from Russia that she had used to polish, the brass warming pan – and some new ones, including a big framed wedding photo of Lynnet and Jonathan.

'The meal will be ready soon,' said Hazel, as she came back in.

'Spotty was a total wet weekend as a guard dog,' said Jandy, as the dog shot through Hazel's legs and settled in front of the fire.

'Oh my God Hazel – you wore an 'at,' said Jandy, when shown the wedding snaps after supper. 'And after all you said!'

Hazel grinned and replied, 'Oh well, sometimes one has to do these things, and it wasn't *too* bad. . .'

Privately Jandy thought it was. 'It doesn't even look like you.'

'No dear, nobody looks like themselves at weddings.' Hazel was really immensely smug. 'Margaret and Alan were exceedingly pleasant to Rex. And after all that sanctimonious tosh a few years ago. Apparently he had a woman in the hotel. Eve, I expect,' she said gleefully; it was one in the eye for Gillian. 'The relations all enjoyed it anyway. . .'

'And the children are calling you Hazel, I hear. Alan thinks it lacks respect.'

'It's a false respect,' asserted Hazel. 'I want them to be ready to take their place in the world, not still abasing themselves before outdated social forms.'

'It sounds too cheeky for words,' Margaret had said to her. 'Hazel this and Hazel that – from your own children.'

'It was passed by the Wicca,' Hazel said lightly.

'That doesn't matter. You should put your foot down.'

'Well Jandy calls you Margaret.'

Margaret subsided, but considered it a low blow.

'I'm getting rather tired of hearing about that Wicca,' she said to Alan. 'It's used as an excuse for everything.'

When they visited the Turners there was a full-blown fuss in progress. Their dog, an appealing mongrel, had like Spotty escaped his chain and taken off across the countryside. He had returned the former evening, but a neighbour was alleging he had served her pedigree bitch. Madeleine was all but in tears, Michael bluff and unapologetic.

'I am not answering ze phone. It may be Mrs 'oward.'

'What on earth do you mean, you're not answering the phone?' demanded Michael, as it continued to ring.

'I mean,' her voice rose, 'I am not answering ze phone, and Michael I tell you if zose bastards are born I go back to Frrrrance.'

Michael's ire was finally roused. 'I've never heard such rot. It's the stupid woman's own fault, she should have kept her precious bitch inside, and I shall tell her so if she rings again. Pull yourself together.'

Margaret and Alan were aghast when Hazel suddenly decided to remove Hebe from the grammar school. 'It's stifling her, I watched it stifle Lynnet, the competitiveness and the self-enclosed all-female flummery.'

'Well that's news to me, that it stifled me,' said an indignant Lynnet. 'And what's wrong with a bit of competitiveness?'

The Barbers backed Lynnet. 'It's political correctness gone mad,' said Alan, 'and you're making Hebe suffer for it.'

'Hebe doesn't feel that way, she wants to leave.'

'Well she shouldn't be given a choice, not at her age,' chipped in Margaret.

There had been some coolness between Hazel and Rex, and little contact. Rex decided he would make the first move, and rang her. His heart dropped when Nick answered. He always felt clumsy with the boy.

'If you've rung to speak to Hazel, she's out. She's standing for parliament,' said Nick.

Rex exploded. 'What!'

It was true. Alan was standing for St. Edfric's Council, for the Conservatives. Not to be outdone, Hazel stood for parliament as the Labour candidate in a nearby constituency. She didn't stand any chance of getting in. The seat was in the old Duke of Grafton's estate, and his steward stood for the Tories.

'All his tenants and tied cottages will turn out to vote. Thank God. I wouldn't stand if there was the remotest chance of getting in,' breezed Hazel gamely.

'Blimey – another terrible 'at.'

Hazel laughed. 'Pop sent it. It's quite an expensive one. You have to wear an 'at, dear, if you stand for parliament. To show you're part of the status quo.'

Back at Windy Ridge Jandy explained to Alan and Margaret, 'She's only standing for a lark.' They exchanged withering glances.

Later in the year, after Hazel didn't get elected and Alan did, they joined forces to condemn the cutting down of the hedgerows. 'It's dreadful,' said Alan, 'some of these hedgerows have been here since the Middle Ages, and they help to drain and water the land. There's often a great ignorance that comes with education – these people think they know better than our ancestors, they don't seem to realise there will be a dust-bowl effect. . .'

'Earth was dying of pollution, for Man was violating his own destiny' began the opening chapter of Rex's 1972 novel *Goodbye Atlantis*. Hazel started up the Farthingale and District Conservation Society. She recruited another teacher from school, and Paul Perkyn and his new lady and her husband, who was changing into a female called Belinda. Margaret and Alan, who had just been co-opted onto the Environmental Committee, were both interested in joining but refused when they heard about Belinda.

The inaugural meeting was held in Moon Farm sitting room, the group voiced their concerns both locally and nationally, and issued a statement condemning the chemical spraying of crops. Mr Harker, the Moon Farm landlord, whose fields lay all about, was amused and took it in his stride, but young Harker was furious. 'You'll have to be careful,' warned Margaret. 'We're very lucky here to have the freedom to say

141

what we think.'

'Freedom is there to be used, not kept on a shelf to admire,' riposted Hazel.

Alan met Jandy at the station, he looked well and slightly plumper under his goatee beard. He loaded her bag into the car and then said without preamble, 'Rex and Hazel are back together again.'

'Whooooooooooppeeeeeeeee,' she replied.

'Oh that's your view, is it? I only marvel how some women never learn.'

'That dreadful man!' said Margaret, of Paul Perkyn. 'Jo was well rid of him.'

'You didn't say that at the time,' pointed out Jandy. 'You blamed Hazel.'

'Yes, because she encouraged Jo to leave her husband.'

'Well logic was never your strong point Margaret, but you're tying yourself into knots with this one.'

'I don't care if I am, I'm not bothered and I'm not going to this wretched meeting with its Belinda or whatever it is.'

The next day Jandy made her way through the old front gate and up the pathway made shadowy by trees. Nick answered the front door at her rap, he gave a grin and bellowed up the stairs, 'Hebe – come down, the working clarse has arrived.' A girl of thirteen, her face full of fun, with masses of honey-coloured hair and a wide red mouth, ran down the stairs enthusiastically.

'She's very good. When I told her Bacon's name she didn't ask where Eggs was,' said Nick.

'That's brilliant. Everybody does. You can be in our Club,' offered Hebe. 'There's just one thing, and if you could do this for us you'd definitely be in.'

'Oh. Do I want to be in your Club, I ask myself.'

'Yes you do. It's about this girl at school, Freya Fitch-Hyslop.'

'Oh not her again.' Hebe had a long-standing war of attrition with her.

'Yes, her. As you know, we don't get on and in her latest exploit she brought a paperback of one of Rex's novels and read out the sex scenes, slowly and loudly to the rest of the school bus. So I told them all she'd had a nanny, that's why she had hang-ups, and she said we'd had a nanny, but I said it was okay because we'd had a marxist nanny. I said it was you.'

'What! You cheeky little things, I'm not your bloody nanny.'

'Well you do look after us sometimes and you have told us about marxism.'

'Yes, when we were barely out of our nappies,' put in Nick.

'. . .So we thought you'd just do us this favour, we thought you wouldn't mind coming to Farthingale Fete and meeting ole Frigga, she'll be there because her mother enters the jam competition every year.'

'Do you know what they've done?' Jandy appealed to Lynnet when she arrived.

Lynnet said in a grand tone, '*Nothing* would surprise me about those two, Hazel doesn't realise what she's given birth to and is happily rearing without a thought for the consequences.'

'We know there's such a thing as sibling jealousy, but you don't have to take it to extremes,' said Nick.

'Well I'm going to bring it up at the next Wicca,' answered Lynnet.

'The Fete's on Saturday and the Wicca is on Sunday, so you'd be too late, Mrs Clever.'

'Okay, what do you want me to wear?' said Jandy resignedly.

'You can wear what you like,' Hebe said generously, 'because you're off-duty.'

Jandy was dragged fruitlessly to Farthingale Fete, as the Fitch-Hyslops sent their jam and went home early. Barny was there, helping with the vintage car display. He stopped, oil and cloth in hand, to give a surly nod. Jasper was playing in the junior football, and Hebe and Nick won a singing competition, with 'White Horses' – perfect for summer, their tender young voices in unison. The Reverend Radice gave out the prizes. Farthingale had hoped Belinda would put in an appearance, but they were disappointed.

The next day it poured with rain, sloshing through gutters and making a mist over the sodden fields. Sunday breakfast was late in the dining room instead of out on the lawn. Afterwards Hazel went to the battered piano in there, to put some vim into the lazy gloomy day, she began playing and everybody in the house gathered round for a sing-song.

'As I cam' through Sandgate
through Sandgate
through Sa-a-andgate
As I cam' through Sandgate
I heard a lassie sing. . .' trebled Hebe.

In a pause, Bacon jumped onto the keys and played her own tune.

At the Wicca in the afternoon Hebe retaliated when Lynnet broached the subject of nannies.

'Well *we* think – and we can easily outvote you – that it's time you and Jonathan had a baby. I want to be an aunt.'

'When we do decide to have a baby I can assure you Hebe that the Wicca is the last place we will consult, and it doesn't matter if you pass it a dozen times,' said an outraged Lynnet, turning and grinning back at Jandy, who was collapsed into laughter.

When Jandy went back to Windy Ridge they were back from their holiday and a family row was in progress. Jasper was refusing to go to a party of one of his schoolfriends.

'Where is the invitation?' demanded Margaret.

Jasper reluctantly growled out, 'I put it in the dustbin.'

'You see Alan, they wanted some boys. . .'

'Yes but why should I be one of them? None of us want to go.'

'Well you're going. And I might tell you that Caroline's father is one of Daddy's best clients.'

'Oh darling, really – how could you? That doesn't matter, he doesn't have to go to her party because of that,' broke in Alan in protest.

'No I know he doesn't darling, I'm not saying such a thing,

I'm just mentioning it that's all.'

'Well I'm not going anyway,' muttered Jasper, settling his jaw in a firm wedge.

'You *are* going. . .'

'Look, I don't even like her. I don't speak to her, I don't have anything to do with her and she doesn't speak to me – I don't know why she wants me at her stupid party.'

'Because her mummy wants the same number of boys as girls.'

'What a bloody silly reason to ask somebody to a party,' said Jandy.

'See – Aunty Jandy agrees with me.'

'Well she doesn't count round here – Alan, tell him.'

'Darling, I don't see why he should go if he doesn't want to,' Alan said mildly. Margaret went berserk.

'He *is* going, he's *going*. He has to learn that he can't treat people in this way. If you didn't want to go you should have said so before.'

'Why don't you just bunk off if you don't want to go,' suggested Jandy helpfully.

'Oh shut up,' replied the child bitterly.

'And when I told all this to Hazel, she agreed with Margaret,' Jandy said wonderingly to Lynnet, who lifted her eyebrows sarcastically and rolled her eyes heavenward.

Margaret Barber to Jandy Lockhart – *September*
My Dear Jandy,

Thank you for your welcome letter and the tam o'shanter – it's a gorgeous colour and quite suits me. Jasper is home from school with a cold so we are having a writing session, so you may get a letter from him too but don't live in hope! We now have 6 turkeys (white) and 41 hens which are just coming in to lay. I have been trying to pot some lavender cuttings, they didn't take well last year so am trying again. We went to St. Edfric's festival this weekend. The highlight was the pageant play and firework display. We took Jasper this year and were most impressed – it was open air in the Abbey gardens, with royal barge and Viking ship coming down the river, all lit up.

Alan has the part of a bear-keeper in this year's pantomime. He has to play a little tune on a recorder – a great worry – it is a peculiar instrument. Christmas soon, the relations are coming down this year – will you come too? I am trying to polish up my table tennis in preparation! This must be all for now, do let us know how you are.

Love from us all,
Margaret

Margaret Barber to Jandy Lockhart – *March*
My Dear Jandy,

We've had so much rain this spring, torrents of it, that the grass and all the children have sprung up suddenly! You'd see such a difference in them. Only Victoria is small, and even she potters about now with a bucket round the pony. Jasper is away at school – he likes it very well. Shane will be sitting his A-levels this year, Hebe & Nick are the same giddy twosome but with longer legs! Alison was at Moon Farm when I called, I hardly recognised her, she is still living in London and working in Cranks a vegetarian restaurant. I've just pulled Sabrina out of the airing cupboard – she loves it in there, if she can sneak in. Must away now and get some jobs done, I hope this finds you well.

All our love, M

Hazel Marlowe to St. Edfric's Free Press – *May*
Dear Sirs/Mesdames,

I would like to bring to the attention of your readers a problem that many of us are experiencing in the lovely countryside of East Anglia. For thousands of years the earth has yielded its riches for the benefit of mankind. Now we have a new factor. I speak of the incessant and over-thorough spraying of crops with strong pesticides, which leaves the fields saturated in chemicals. How can this be a good thing when the resultant crops are to be consumed by humans? Walking from the bus-stop past the fields after spraying had taken place I felt quite faint. Last night Weston, Farthingale & Farthingale Inferior Conservation Society passed a resolution condemning over-zealous crop-spraying, and calling on the Ministry of Agriculture to exercise tighter government controls on its supervision.

> Yours sincerely,
> Hazel Marlowe

Margaret Barber to Jandy Lockhart – *May*
My Dear Jandy,

Hazel has had her photo in the paper, the Free Press descended and took her by surprise with a photographer. She doesn't like the photo but was pleased about the article because it's more publicity for the anti-crop spraying bunch. Alan and I support them but he says there is a way of doing things which can be more effective, and is to bring it up on the Environmental Committee. The weather is very wet and windy still and spring seems to be passing quickly. The baby birds have flown from the thrushes' and sparrows' nests in the conifers, I have just finished making a lamp from an empty sherry bottle and stones we collected from Dunwich beach last summer. It's almost time to collect Victoria from nursery so must away. Try to ring me.

> Fondest love,
> Margaret

Lynnet Reed to Jandy Lockhart – *September*
Dear Jandy,

How's things? You probably heard – we're living in Ticehurst. It's a nice village and not too far for Jonathan to commute. I'm having driving lessons – a car is a necessity in such an out of the way place, and as I shall probably always be living in remote places I do need to drive. I am now learning to be a hausfrau! I was at Farthingale last week – Hazel & Margaret were bent over their pans and stirring like something out of Macbeth using a recipe from my Gran (suffragette chutney?). Drop me a line and let me know how you are.

Love,
Lynnet

Margaret Barber to Jandy Lockhart – *October*
My Dear Jandy,

I am grabbing a moment to write a quick letter as Alan has gone off with Michael, to rehearsals – the pair of them are in the pantomime chorus again. Daddy is out too, he is locum today. Mr Huggins's dog killed two of our bantams, so we only have one now, she flew up into a tree. She was a bit lost at first but the day after the killing laid her first egg for about twelve months! She still lays the occasional one. There has been a bumper apple crop this year, the shops in Farthingale and Thetford have big baskets of them outside with notices PLEASE HELP YOURSELF (so you are wrong – it isn't only Cuba where they give away surplus stuff). The thing is – what to do with them. Hazel and myself have been storing them wrapped individually in newspaper, and she has a super recipe from her mother for chutney so we've both been giving it a go. If I'm not in when Mr Chew comes he leaves the greengrocery box on the kitchen table plus lots of apples I don't want.

Tom Feetham had a nasty do – he knocked Alan's father up in the middle of the night having crawled two miles from the village with an asthma attack. He gave the poor chap an injection and got the car out and drove him home. Daddy's curtains were closed until late the next day so we knew something had gone off.

In the afternoons I go with Victoria to feed Blue – he is in his winter stabling now, the McGeehans have let us have a stable until we can make a paddock for him here.

Another job! What's happening to you – are you still going to your Indian dance classes? Let us know.

Fondest love,
Margaret

Hazel Marlowe to Jandy Lockhart – *March*
Dear Jandy,

Well here we are – it's nearly spring once more and the sap is rising, and after digging me peas and beans in – I hope to drown in veg this summer – I'm now writing to you at last. Well how are things? Been on any more picket lines? Lynnet is gynormous – I'll be surprised if she goes until August – she's getting v. cheesed off – off her food and can't imbibe the grape – she plans a right royal rave up after delivery. She's been round with Margaret, they've been cutting out patterns together and sewing maternity clothes. Lynnet wants to continue afterwards too, preparing for a world bankrupt of energy, esp. if there are problems with fuel, if the miners decide to go on strike. Shane is hugely enjoying his second term at Cambridge, he came home at Christmas and his friends came in the New Year. We had a big party, Lynnet cooked one of her splendiferous Victorian meals and we all dressed up appropriately. Alan came as Mr Micawber and the Victorian manner suited him! Nick is helping me with the vegetable patch and has started a kitten exchange register. Hebe is into painting and pottery. Hazel does her nut: Let's be hearing from you – are you coming down soon?

Love,
Hazel

Lynnet's baby was born in August. That month too the Revolution is Now movement – five earnest young people and an agent provocateur – threw a bomb at the car of a cabinet minister. Within the week they were arrested, their names all over the national press. One of them was Miriam Blumenthal.

Hazel's sister Helen rang through after six o'clock to say this was Harry Blumenthal's daughter.

'Season's Greetings to all at Moon Farm, from Harry & Sheila, Mary & Sarah' the card read each year.

The Barbers were aghast, Lynnet vociferously against, Jandy called it romantic opportunism.

Hazel and Jandy were out by the big barn picking blackberries to make a tart for tea. 'I've offered to have Miriam while she's on bail, and they've submitted she would be staying with an old friend of the family in the country,' said Hazel. 'Being in the Spanish Civil War, Harry was such a hero to us, and there's something about a hero that you can't touch, you can't contact. I wonder if it was like that for Miriam – she uses that name now, not Mary – when she was growing up. That perhaps she felt alienated from her father's past but wanted to live up to it.'

'Hmmmm,' mused Jandy uncertainly.

'Margaret and Alan are being very stuffy. I think it annoys people when somebody acts decisively. It reminds them that they themselves have forgotten how to respond directly to injustice. It makes them defensive of their own inactivity, they envy the ability to take action. Without defending what she did, I think it's a commendable instinct in the young which we should value.'

Jandy herself already felt twinges of jealousy at the idea of this unknown girl who went forward and did something, she didn't 'lapse forever into a classic fatigue' which had been Jandy's bugbear when she lived at Farthingale. 'Well what they did was pretty stupid. None of the rest of the Left would touch them with a bargepole. What's democratic about a bomb, for Godsake?' she answered, dropping berries like dark jewels into the pudding basin.

'Do you think I'm wrong, then?' asked Hazel, uncharacteristically hesitant.

'No. You're absolutely right. You could really help her,' responded Jandy fervently.

'Well that's what I hope for.'

After tea she said, 'Come and see the bedsit I've made for her.'

Miriam was due to arrive at the end of the summer, and Hazel had prepared the front sitting room. She had put fresh silver moonpods in the bay window, clean linen on the bed-settee, and moved the rug over a stain in the carpet where Shane had dropped chemicals when it had been his room. The old utility sideboard was moved into a corner and made empty to accommodate Miriam's things. A few books were laid on the bedside table – Elaine Morgan's *'The Descent of Woman'* and the essays of Jung and D.H.Lawrence; a print of Breughel's 'The Fall of Icarus' was pinned to the wall. The room was shadowed by swaying leaves, the chestnut branches through the side window and the trees in the front garden.

'Well I'll support you whatever you decide to do,' Rex said over the telephone, still faithful to the commitment made together in their youth. 'Is she definitely coming, then?'

'It's not definite yet. It depends on the bail conditions. Helen said Sheila and the other daughter are taking it badly. I don't know about Harry.'

'I don't hear from him now – not for years,' Rex replied, remembering their jaunt together when Hazel was in the hospital giving birth. 'Isn't she a few months younger than Lynnet? You and Sheila were pregnant at the same time?'

'Yes. Lynnet isn't supportive at all, I'm afraid.'

It was true. Lynnet railed against 'spoiled students who thought they were entitled to their own way.'

'Yes, but they live in a very self-enclosed world at university, it was Sussex – an absolute hotbed of activity, and it's obvious the lecturers had just blown these kids' minds.'

'Oh that's right – blame the lecturers. . .'

'Well now Hazel, I'm afraid Lynnet's right about this. Thank goodness at least one of your children has some sense,' said Alan. 'Of course we all want to help the people we know, but where do you draw the line?'

'Is nobody then to be given a second chance?' Hazel cried passionately. 'Many young people have strong opinions – what about you – you were attracted to fascism, you mixed with fascists, at one time your opinions were very extreme but nobody held it against you,' she stormed.

'Oh Hazel, you do exaggerate,' said Alan, really quite hurt. 'It's true I had some. . . some. . . different opinions, and I still do think usury should be monitored, but planting bombs is in another category – it undermines civilisation,' he protested.

'Yes well you might point that out to the Americans in Vietnam,' riposted Hazel crushingly, before sweeping off in a dudgeon.

'Honestly!' steamed Margaret after she had gone. 'Trust Hazel – "Is no one to be given a second chance" – that's just like these blasted liberals.'

'I don't think Hazel would thank you for calling her a liberal,' Jandy pointed out.

Miriam didn't come and the room, the honesty, the books and all the little preparations left Hazel with a sense of loss. The house seemed empty, echoing, the voices of the children slightly unreal to her, as though far away. . . Yet she had been here before, couldn't think when. . . Yes. It was Withy House after the loss of the baby. All prepared and ready, a tabernacle awaiting an arrival.

'Good heavens Hazel – whatever's wrong? You look terrible,' burst in Margaret, concerned.

5

WINTER

In late autumn Jandy was back in Farthingale, unable to speak. She had discharged herself from the mental hospital and Andrew had put her on the five o'clock boat-train to Harwich, calling at St. Edfric's.

She sat on Nottingham station, waiting for the train. Drizzle fell lightly, in the distance lights against the dark, nearby a muted station light and she watched steam rise from it as the drizzle fell. The sounds of the station, trains hissing and clanging, disembodied voices across the platform. Then the station spoke. 'Nottingham. This is Nottingham. Nottingham. . . echoed about in the darkness. It was the most beautiful voice she had ever heard, iced sweetness in the night, and tears dropped from her at the loveliness of the sound. He put her on the train and fastened the compartment door and lifted a hand to her slowly as the train pulled out.

The journey was darkness and rhythm and thankfully solitude. Few travellers got on the boat train on a Sunday evening and they went into other compartments. Saliva cascaded uncontrollably from the corner of her mouth, and she held a tissue to it, which she kept having to renew. Her life had turned to darkness and joltings and the unknown. Alan met her at St. Edfric's and took her case and the cat basket.

Windy Ridge was all closed up for the winter, they lived

mostly in the cosy little room next to the kitchen, with its brick fireplace and big lined curtains pulled across the door to the sitting room, the television wheeled into a corner and constantly on. Jasper was away at school, Victoria in bed by the time they arrived. Later that evening Moll Flanders was shown on television, Julia Foster's broken face riding to prison, rocking carriage and ringlets and utter despair. 'I'll get better. I'll get out of this,' she wept and Jandy reflected that back and saw how Moll's life did improve and she held onto it, that it would happen to her too.

The next day Dr Barber came in. 'She can't speak, she's having to write everything down,' said Margaret.

'I see. Her mind is all right, I think. You can understand me, can't you?'

Jandy nodded but couldn't move the muscles on her face which had gone rigid, like a statue.

'I'm afraid it will probably be a question of time and patience,' he said. But the next day he went off to a luncheon given by drugs companies, held every other month, and followed by a lecture. He brought the menu back, for them to see – rainbow trout and french fried potatoes, followed by lemon mousse. Jandy handled it as carefully as she could. 'And you'll never believe what the lecture was about,' he said, animated. 'It was the treatment of patients with a bad reaction to Moditen – which is what you were given. So there we are. You don't need to worry any more, because we know what to do, and I have never seen anything quite so fortuitous.'

In the mornings she went for long walks in the wood or lanes, her spine jumping all the time. Among the upturned fields lay a thousand shattered pieces of shadow; blank sky shone back in the water between the mud of bike tracks. Ravens picked among loose uncollected corn. The hedgerows held hips and a few bright leaves – solitary ornaments among the old man's beard and spider webs. Seeing the late berries, spattered with devil's spit, and the clawing dead arms of the brambles, she thought of a year ago, picking blackberries for tea, Hazel wondering what to do about Miriam, berries like dark jewels hitting the cream basin. . . a world, an eternity away.

154

Hazel came. 'Hello Jandy, what are you doing here – you're a summer phenomenon.' Inside her head: 'No it's all you who belong to the summer.' She couldn't swallow so Margaret made soups, and put her to work lining the drawers in the kitchen. 'You have to *make* yourself keep going.' She absorbed everything, offered no resistance. She set the table and passively watched the warm lights on the china, sending forth a glow into the dim winter afternoon, reflected in the glass of the French doors and superimposed onto the dripping garden. The china sparkled pink and white and wreathed with flowers and berries, the tea things all set out, an order upon all, the same each day. In the kitchen the rack of golden sponge cakes, cooling from the oven and waiting to be put onto a cake plate. Dr Barber came into the kitchen from his rounds and a smile lit his face when he saw the sombreros, as he called them. 'Aren't they lovely?' he remarked to Jandy. 'I always think there must be a little Mexican asleep under each one, having his siesta.'

The afternoon tea now was a fixed point in an uncertain world, precarious, precious.

She peered into the vase cupboard, full of empty vessels, shadowed and undisturbed: different sizes, stone jars and glass, mock Chinese; the pale green vase that always held anemones, part of the order of the seasons and of routine that made their life so solid. After making her careful poised arrangements Margaret always put the leftover flowers in a jamjar and stood it in the pantry window, reluctant to cast away their short little lives. Most vases unused late in the year, there were paper flowers in the hall and in a brass jug plump hips and twigs frosted with fake ice in the small sitting room.

The Christmas decorations went up, Margaret iced the cake assisted by Victoria. Jasper returned from school. 'What's wrong with your face?' he demanded.

'Aunty Jandy isn't very well darling.'

'She just kicked me,' he complained.

On Christmas Eve Jasper went off to play football for the village, and Andrew visited and took Jandy and Victoria for tea at the Angel, crumpets and cakes in front of the fire, Victoria talking non-stop.

The December fields lay under white sky unmarked by cloud; stems of straying smashed barley, bent into a horizon of mud, the pieces of shadow in the ploughed fields like the upturned fragments of a nether world. The Great Dane followed them through the wood slowly, and then surged ahead galloping, the air as though trapped between his large legs and he rode it seemingly in slow motion.

That winter gales whipped about the land, bringing down cables and trees, charging into fences and barns. The wind buffeted about and drove along the exposed road to Farthingale, which now had but depleted hedgerow and a few trees. The road to Thelnetham was more winding and sheltered, but it too received a thrashing. Across the narrow road lay twigs and limbs of trees brought down, or they hung from the trees held in air by the clutching ivy. Behind wooden barns stock breathed all together, clouds of heat and moisture, closing their brown eyes slowly and opening them, rubbing leather shoulder to shoulder, ears bent listening to the storms.

There was a New Year party at the Barbers. Margaret made Chicken Marengo and spare ribs and profiteroles, and insisted Jandy make a gugelhupf. In her mind she was saying 'A gugelhupf, for Godsake, I don't cook at the best of times, let alone make a bloody gugelhupf. . .'

Margaret, seeing her look, said, 'You've got to *make* yourself.'

All came from Moon Farm except Shane who was recovering from 'flu. Hazel's parents were down for the holidays and they came too. Dr Barber sat talking to Mrs Grove, and Nick and Jasper played table tennis. Helen Grove showed her film slides of that year's summer holiday and of the Marlowe children when very small.

Storms banged across the land and the entire area was cut off electricity. Jandy decamped in a huff to Moon Farm because an ex-boyfriend wanted to visit her. 'No. Alan's putting his foot down, Andrew's always welcome of course but absolutely no to any more. Have you finished with Andrew?'

In a temper Jandy wrote: 'Yes and I've finished with

Rocco as well.'

'Oh my heavens, I don't understand any of it.'

So when Rocco turned up she slammed off in his car.

Hebe, Nick and Roger went for a walk in the gale, and came back with a motorist in the dark wild night, stuck because a tree had fallen across the road. He was an American from the base, and was cross-questioned and required to play a game of Frazzle, before being given a milk drink and candle and a bed. Rocco and Jandy put on their coats and Hazel asked, 'Has everyone in this house gone mad? This lot are just back from a midnight walk and now you two are off. . .'

As February set in Shane had another bout of 'flu, and was unable to return to Cambridge. Jandy, who was talking by now although very thin, stayed with him whilst Hazel was at school. With the power off and the house cold, Hazel dragged the mattress from Shane's bed onto the sitting room floor, and the coal fire was kept going night and day.

In the late afternoon dusk before the daylight went Hazel and Jandy filled the brass paraffin lamps, Hebe started the tea and Nick piled up the coal scuttle and chopped wood. Shane lay prostrate on the mattress. In the daytime Jandy heated soup or beans for them both and made lots of hot drinks, and they played Scrabble together, the board on the floor by his elbow. They kept pausing in the game to give themselves a rest and have another hot drink. 'I always hope to put out the word syzygy,' said Jandy. 'I haven't ever managed it yet.'

'What does it mean?' asked the boy.

'I can't remember, but it makes me think of Hazel and Rex.'

He leaned over to pull at the dictionary. 'It means,' he read slowly, 'a yoked pair, or the conjunction and opposition of two heavenly bodies, especially in the case of the moon with the sun.'

He shut the book with the faintest of grey smiles, wan but amused. Then he lay back, exhausted, worn with cares.

'I don't think I want to play any more. I'm tired,' he said.

Jandy collected the pots and went to the kitchen to wash them. The fire crackled and spat, Shane slept and Jandy read Russian short stories on the old plum velvet sofa that had taken so many buffetings during the Marlowe children's growing up. Shane had ridden among the cushion-donkeys as a little boy at Withy House, as babies they had all wet on it, Hebe and Nick had fished with string over the back, adolescent Lynnet had fallen asleep on it, mouth open, whilst Hazel and Jandy had talked all night until the dawn chorus; Jo Perkyn had sat on it to tell her dreams to Hazel.

As Shane slept Jandy made up the fire as silently as possible and then went to look through the window. The garden was forlorn, the sky endlessly white.

Hazel sailed in after school in mid-afternoon. 'How is he?' she asked anxiously, dropping her watch loosely into the dish, discarding Time.

'He's been no fun today,' complained Jandy, 'he wouldn't play Scrabble any more.' She went off when Alan called for her, and the long evening settled in at Moon Farm, light juddering round the lamps, pooling into dark corners. The gloom decreed early bedtimes for all, and Hebe and Nick packed themselves off with candles and water bottles and hot drinks. Hazel stoked up the fire and decided to sleep on the old sofa, to be near Shane.

As the night wore on he grew delirious, raved and rambled and muttered, and threw off the bedclothes. Sometimes he was lucid. 'You don't understand. You don't see me as I am. You think I'm perfect. You've always thought that. I'm not perfect. You expect so much. . . I can't live up to it. . .'

She felt his brow, restored the bedcovers, sat stroking his hair. 'No, no. It's all right, it's all right, we don't expect anything more from you. . .'

In the morning she telephoned the doctor, and when he came he rang for an ambulance.

At the hospital it was touch and go. Shane was put into intensive care. Rex was summoned. He ran straight to his car and drove up, passing through traffic lights and unheeding road signs. When he entered the hospital and saw Hazel, haggard and distraught, her face scored with lines, he knew he had never loved her so much, had never felt so bound to her. She had had to cope with this all by herself in the middle of the country, without a car.

He and Hazel stayed at the hospital together all the time, never leaving the bedside. The illness of their golden child reduced everything else to the category of irrelevant.

At Windy Ridge Alan reflected on when he was in the West Suffolk hospital recovering from the bull, Rex visited and told him of Shane's birth. Alan had never seen him so jubilant. He himself was at a low point, lying in a hospital bed – for who cared about him, that he was ill, or whether he recovered? Rex ecstatic, truly at a high moment in his life. And now. . . poor Shane lay in the West Suffolk near death. They hadn't met for years, but he felt Rex's distress.

Hazel and Rex had a reconciliation over the hospital bed. Shane, the favourite; the perfect, the child who was the least trouble, even Rex stood in awe of his knowledge of science. The boy who had his own bedroom-laboratory at the age of eight, that no one was allowed to enter without his permission. Shane – named for the man who stood alone in the untamed golden West; the boy who replaced the baby son who died. . .

When at last he was starting to recover Hazel and Rex embarked on a last heady romantic fling. 'Yes, go and enjoy yourselves, I'll be fine now,' he said to them with a smile.

In the car Hazel, taut for so long, leaned back and left everything to him. 'Where do you want to eat?' he enquired. She shook her head, wordless and compliant, basking in his strength.

6

SUMMER

That year was the last true Moon Farm summer. All around the garden bloomed, the flowers smiled, Hazel was bright-eyed and happy, Rex much in evidence since the resumption of their affair. Shane was back at Cambridge. Hebe and Nick were now lively teenagers, Lynnet at Moon Farm with her toddler, her marriage on the rocks. Poor old Spot was becoming arthritic, but still managed on occasion to escape and tear over the countryside to fulfil his masculine destiny.

Hazel, newly learned to drive, took them all to the old aerodrome invisible among the corn. She alone knew where she was going. They swept around a concrete ramp and she stopped the car in the middle of the corn. 'If anywhere should be haunted, it's this place,' she said dreamily, surveying the Suffolk afternoon adrift in blue and clouds.

The hangars were weed encrusted, silent; the wind which stirred the grass made no sound. Inside they found emptiness and slabs of concrete floor, the roof missing in chunks. As deserted as any Roman camp, abandoned when the Eagle called their return over a thousand years ago. Sightseers and archaeologists worry those places, but here all was still, no evidence of living left. No bar or kitchen or privy, the lockers all gone. All that was left was the wooden frame and the idea of the airmen. Some of the rafters were down, and between splintered wood smudged government posters embedded in the walls still announced 'Careless Talk Costs LIVES'.

Hazel seemed to hold her breath with wonder, remembering when everything in the world was threatened. The others went round poking their big fingers into everything and making jokes. Hazel replied but was almost trancelike, back in the time of burning skies and charred pieces of her earth. Dwarfed now by sons and shouted down by daughters, her babies lost in these big people, for her the air here was thick with the presence of men who went off into the night and never came back. Their shadows lay across the land – defenders, fathers, lovers and now sons to her, she as though in her youth.

Over the rubble lay dead webs and sunlight so still it seemed reflected from the past. They crashed through the hollow rooms yet the clangour of young voices didn't make any impression on the dense silence. Cable like sheathed tendons spilled down the prefab walls from a black box whose meter has ticked by nothings for years, dial rusted, hands as locked and dead as a crusader's since the last light was switched out forever.

Hazel laughed. 'When we came in the spring,' she said, 'a little bird had made her nest on top of that box. And she didn't mind us a bit, she just sat there on her eggs.' Her eyes shine at the recollection, as they had used to shine before her small children. ('Well I must go and be a mother,' she would say, pretending detachment, yet eyes alive with delight.) She turned to have her pleasure confirmed, her joy at the fact of this other small mother. Gaiety enters the party. They step lightly, easily, shadows seem benign now. Between the ruptured floorboards and the spill of debris lies a bird, claws outstretched, eyes and beak fast shut, wing wide and stiff. All gather, sorry and questioning. Some remember the little brown bird in the spring, getting on with her own affairs.

'Why?' 'Why?' 'Why?' reverberates around the empty shell. 'Why? – for nothing,' – her voice drags with grief. 'For nothing.' Once more her faith in the universe is shattered.

Rex Marlowe to the *Sussex Gazette* – *September*
Dear Sirs,

The recent suggestion from one of your correspondents that Elizabeth I was a tyrant is arrant nonsense. At a time when thousands of people in continental Europe – Spain, France, parts of the Netherlands – were on funeral pyres, condemned by the Inquisition as heretics because of their beliefs, Elizabeth wrote 'I have no wish to open up a window into men's souls' – in other words, her subjects were free to think as they liked. Our country has gained immeasurably from that freedom of thought, and even now four centuries later we are still living in the benign golden shadow of the Faerie Queen herself.

Yours faithfully,

Rex Marlowe

Rex visited and told them London was unbearable, 'sizzling and stifling, bits of bare bodies everywhere, it's like a charnel-house, or a hot mediaeval summer when we were part of the continent.' This summer Rex came often and didn't feel excluded by the gaiety at Moon Farm, it chimed with his own lightheartedness because Shane was safe.

Nick went off in the early mornings to work in the Simmses vineyard on the other side of Thankful. The spectacular heat, so welcome, increased, intensified, the grass burnt, the air grew thick with stupefaction.

At breakfast Hazel announced, 'I don't care what the government says, I watered the poor garden earlier on, so will you all please use as little water as possible today.'

It was like a dream, the land tinderbox dry. In some parts of the country there were reports of ladybird plagues. The meteorological office at nearby Mildenhall reported that the heat would continue, and there were forty-four continuous days without rain.

'This is the potty potter,' – Hazel introduced a spotty youth with long hair and an affable expression.

'Hello,' said Jandy.

'Five white mice,' replied Badger, relishing her look of confusion.

'Don't you mean three blind mice?'

'Oh no, I mean five white mice or six pickled squirrels.'

Hazel was smiling and Hebe looked vague but pleased. Presumably she was used to this form of social exchange as she had started working at the pottery some of the time. Jandy smiled – she had fulfilled her social obligations and greeted him and promptly forgot about him for the rest of her stay.

There was only one sadness in the rejoicing of that summer – the house-martins hadn't returned from Africa. Their little mud-houses were still crusted above the bedroom window but the nests had been empty all summer.

The weather finally broke at the end of September. It was still warm, but the summer was over. The Marlowes prepared for a Farewell Summer dinner party.

'So we'll all meet up here in twenty years time. That's September 1996,' instructed Hebe, and all round the table assented, for none of them believed with any conviction that such a date would ever occur. Candlelight trembled on the plates and pooled their faces onto the dark panes of the windows. The tabby cat jumped onto the open piano and walked along the yellow keys, playing her own tune, the young faces bent forward into the light, conspiring, planning, eager. The smell of the hot food they were eating wafted about; beyond the side window in the night lay the empty orchard, the abandoned peg-basket waist high in wet grass, apples fallen and forgotten.

Shane's friend Roger told anecdotes to Jandy, Hazel and Alison argued the merits of cold baked beans in salads, and Joy, Hebe's friend from two fields away, described to Alan her designs for the signpost that Thankful Village Council had decided to commission. Lynnet, Shane and Steve, the American dragged in from the February storms, listened to Philip, imprisoned inside a new black beard, telling about his holiday in a Yugoslavian village. Hebe, eighteen now, carefully bathed and anointed and wearing a topaz necklace against her throat, wore her honey-coloured hair caught back in a barrette

163

and looked suddenly rather grown-up. Nick had brought Jenny Simms, from the vineyard. Old Spotty looked up, faintly curious but untroubled, from under the sideboard.

The empty casserole was removed. Jonathan, visiting on a truce with Lynnet, replenished everybody's wine. On the sideboard, under a jug of honesty and fairy lanterns, were hot mincemeat turnovers and a pot of cream. Hebe had made the mincemeat, setting to like a chemist in the kitchen, weighing and chopping and churning the lot together with a big wooden spoon.

Upstairs Lynnet's toddler woke and hollered and was brought down. 'Elizabeth – why all these tears? Look darling – here's Chomsky,' waving a ragged teddy bear – 'he's sitting here on the piano all the time, enjoying the fun. . .' The baby was taken out to pick silver pennies from the honesty in the dark front garden.

Outside, all along the road to Farthingale, cloud multitudes teemed and turned and smoked their way across the dark heavens, the fields under them silent, awed.

After the plates had been cleared away Hazel seated herself at the piano and Hebe and Nick were induced to sing together. Roger recited a poem in Latin, which he assured everyone was very moving as it was a funeral ode, and then, to great acclaim, Steve gave forth from memory 'Barbara Freitchie' – ' "Shoot if you must this old grey head, but spare your country's flag" she said. . .'

Alison and Jandy came in from the kitchen and Irish coffee was handed round between the starry candlelight. Afterwards, they were going to clear the table and ask the glass about the Future.

7

FESTIVAL

Alan met Jandy at the station. He loaded her bag into the car and started up. 'Are you all prepared for the Festival?' she asked.

'Yes, well, I hope so. At the last minute some committee decided the hanging baskets must come down, in case they fall on somebody's head. I don't understand how they make these rules. We prevailed on them to wait until after the Festival.'

He drove in a spin about the outer narrow streets of St. Edfric's, and Jandy caught quick snatches of petunias and church steeples, before the main road swept away into the countryside.

'Did you know,' said Alan, 'it's been recently found that a document was drawn up for St. Edfric's in February 1215, granting full rights to citizens and burghers within the gates, with the royal seal and the signature of the abbot. Of course, you realise what that shows?' he said meaningfully, guiding the car through the Suffolk lanes, the waving young corn, the endless summer sky ahead, toward the everlasting curve of the world.

'What does it mean?' asked Jandy obligingly.

'It means that *we* had Magna Carta first. Before it was signed at Runnymede in June.'

He kept his eyes on the road and didn't turn as she let out a peal of laughter. As the car turned from the Farthingale road she cast a look, as of old, across the fields to where Moon Farm stood, between haystacks and barns, its gables and windows and chimneys from this distance the same as ever, but the house empty. Hazel had died, the children flown away to new lives.

'Don't you know anything about that period?' he quizzed critically.

'Geoffrey Fitzurse,' she replied, endeavouring to appear intelligent.

'Why him?'

'It's the only name I remember from the Middle Ages.'

At Windy Ridge – an absurd name, it was built in a sheltered field – Margaret was waiting with laid table. She was in a wheelchair now, but whizzed round in it and still did the cooking, and sewed tapestries.

Round the table the talk was of the Festival and of the Barbers' recent visit to France, to the town – suitably mediaeval – twinned with St. Edfric's. Speaking French with ease, he and Margaret had gone over with a good will delegation.

Margaret was animated, in spite of the wheelchair, 'It was Alan's suggestion they ask Yehudi Menuhin to play at the Festival. He remembered when Hazel used to treat us to Lavenham each year. . .'

Some of the Marlowes were coming to the Abbey, Helen would be driving down from Manchester with Nick and his wife, and Lynnet. Lynnet was divorced now with two little girls and taking Archaeology at Manchester. After Hazel's death Nick had joined a religious community and then married young. Jandy listened to Margaret tell of their doings, although she and Lynnet kept in touch. Hebe had stayed in Cambridge after her degree, and Shane was in America measuring the spaces between stars.

Jasper, now a cheerful printer, called in to see them. His red hair was darker now, his arms burnished gold where the hair grew thick. He lived in a nearby village but still played football for the Thankful team. Victoria was newly married and living elsewhere.

Later she settled into the little back room she had used when she lived there. It had hardly changed. The midnight lace wedding dress still hung in the spare cupboard, and there was the window where Sabrina the Beautiful would appear, mouse pendant from her jaws, her dark moon eyes bringing the night in with her.

On the dressing table stood old scent bottles and powder bowl and photo of Dr Barber – now long in the churchyard after a happy and useful life. She always looked for Rex's first book, from that early happy summer, the first summer of the marriage – 'To Alan & Margaret, hoping they find their own Tomorrow's Gift – Rex' – his handwriting powerful and uncompromisingly male.

She sipped her tea. The world she lived in was so different, her own life seemed here inauthentic, but she had long ago realised there was nothing she could do to make her life authentic to Margaret. More intransigent these days, Margaret seemed to have lost the quality she had of suddenly on the crest of indignation seeing the funny side.

Outside the window in the dark the trees sighed, and beyond the hedgerow mist lay over the moonlit wheat. She remembered when this was the favourite field, before the house was built. Closing the window against the night and against memories, she took in every detail of the room before it became a dream too.

Once in bed, she recalled the last joyful summer of 1976. By the following year the serpent had got in, in the form of Badger. He took over Moon Farm, he challenged Hazel – both actually and by default and a process of decay had started. The adolescent serpent. Hazel had no defences, although nobody realised it at the time, least of all Badger, who wasn't aware of the thin ground he stood on.

In that summer Hebe absconded with Badger to Dunwich, they were together in a beach hut. Hazel was worried. 'I'm going to get her back. Will you come with me?'

'Is that a good idea?'

'She's had glandular fever and there's this Hepatitis B virus going about now, I'm not satisfied that she's taking enough care. Hepatitis B can be very serious. And how can she be concentrating on her work? She's had an offer for Cambridge but she won't get in if she fritters her time away with him. . .'

'Oh, okay,' said Jandy unenthusiastically.

Nick grinned. 'What do you think's going to happen? They aren't going to row or anything.'

Jandy had only ever seen Dunwich on snaps – showing a merry party of Farthingalers on the dunes; Margaret tickling baby Jasper's toes; Hazel and kids around a teapot, Jo spreading butter. Every summer when the children were small they all went there together, or on overlapping visits.

'She's only nineteen!' burst forth from Hazel, 'and she's young for her age. She's completely innocent, she's lived in the country. . .'

'I was fifteen when I met Andrew, Lynnet was seventeen when she was involved with Paul Perkyn, Margaret was eighteen when I was born. And Rex was eighteen when you first met.'

Hazel bridled at this, said, 'Yes. But we waited until the War was over. In those days people had some self-control, they didn't expect to have something just because they wanted it.'

Jandy shrugged, washing her hands of it. She had no opinion of Badger, he didn't look a lot of use in the class struggle, but that can be said of many persons.

The next day they drove to Ipswich for Hazel to attend a meeting of the West Suffolk Education Committee. It lasted over an hour, and then they got back into the car and set off for Dunwich. It was a while before either spoke, knowing a disagreement loomed ahead. Hazel had been co-opted onto the education committee after the union representative was taken ill. Now her year was nearly over the union organiser had approached her after the meeting to say, 'Mrs Marlowe, we'd be perfectly happy for you to continue as our candidate.' This had enraged Hazel for some deep-seated reason, she snapped back she would stand as an independent.

168

She kept her eyes on the road, and when she spoke it took Jandy by surprise. 'It's no good. You haven't fought me.'

'*Fought* you!' yelped out Jandy, astonished.

'Yes. You'll fight me about little things like the unions. . .'

'*Little* things! That isn't a little thing. . .'

'But it is little to you, it's not personal, it's just part of a political programme.'

'I'm amazed at such petit-bourgeois tripe. Hazel, you've just sat round a committee table and voted on every single issue with the union or the way the union would have voted, but you've always got to be difficult, haven't you, you've always got to be awkward.'

'I'm not being told what to do by the union,' she replied belligerently.

'That's misunderstanding what a union is. The unions are at the heart of democracy. One man one vote – and in the workplace too. Look at the miners – they are the diamonds in the crown. A miner – an amazing fabled being who goes deep down into the earth, and can say No if he chooses. How else could it be in a free society?'

In spite of herself Hazel started to smile, at home with the swing of the words and something inside her pleased at them. 'Oh that's just rhetoric,' she said lightly.

'You sound like Margaret and Alan. They don't know any better, but you – you're from Manchester, the city of Friedrich Engels and the Pankhursts, and it's disgraceful in your case.'

'Yes dear.'

'Voting in a union is the epitome of democracy, not its negation. You won't get anywhere without the organised working-class. . .'

'No and you won't get anywhere without the middle-class either,' snapped back Hazel. 'They set the agenda in this country, both historically and now. All the gains we have were initiated by the middle-class – an end to the slave trade, prison reform, the right to vote. . .'

'So instead of standing as the union candidate you're going to stand as an independent and get defeated!'

'That's right. There are worse things than being defeated.'

h

'Playing lose-'ems. That's what you accuse me of.'

'You do play lose-'ems.'

'Then I must have learnt it from you.'

'You always sound very certain Jandy, but in the essentials you are passive. With Margaret. And with Andrew.'

'I've just left Andrew.'

'Nevertheless you have a long history of passivity where he is concerned. That's probably why you have affairs,' continued Hazel, her eyes on the road ahead. 'I fought Rex but I didn't need to have affairs because we were equals.'

'It didn't seem to work the other way round,' replied Jandy before she could stop herself.

Hazel said coolly, 'No. It didn't.' They drove quietly for a while, then Hazel said, 'I expect you'll go back to Andrew. You always do.'

'Not this time. I'm in love.'

Sick of the sound of the word and its use as an excuse for crazy behaviour, Hazel said nothing, turned the car into the coast road and the fire between them died down.

When they arrived at Dunwich the two teenagers were quite keen to see them, Hebe made them coffee. The beach house was pleasant and clean, there were a few books on a shelf and white ghost-faced axolotls swimming about in a tank. 'How absolutely weird.'

Over the coffee Hazel broached the reason for the visit. 'I want you to come back with me to Moon Farm.'

Badger frowned and looked razor-eyed at Hebe, who seemed vague. 'You know yourself that you aren't well. . .'

'But Badger isn't well either,' objected Hebe.

'Well,' said Hazel, with her wonderful benevolent smile, 'I think they both need looking after, don't you? I think we should take them both back to Moon Farm.'

Jandy, aware that she had been unceremoniously dragooned as one of Hazel's heavies – a role that didn't sit easily with her careless nature – smiled non-committally.

'We'll go and have a walk on the beach while you talk it over,' said Hazel, as always in command.

'It looks as though Badger is going to try to persuade her to stay,' she remarked, as they wandered along the sands.

'Would that be so bad?'

'Glandular fever can be very serious. It's Hebe's health I'm concerned with. And how is she going to get into Cambridge, messing about down here and wasting her time?'

Jandy nodded.

'I could see Badger is going to pressurise her as soon as we left. If he has prevailed, then all I can do is to appeal to his better nature. . .'

The coast was distant, it was crumbling away, it might be gone in their lifetimes. Seabirds whirled and called above their heads, Kessingland signposted in the dunes. 'I went there ages ago. To a camp,' said Jandy. 'Summer of '71.' Only six years before, it seemed another age. 'The summer Lynnet was married.'

'Oh yes, well that's in a mess. Did you see the way Badger looked at me? He's absolutely hostile.'

'Well now, what have you two decided?' The prevarication in the air that was Hebe's, and the hostility emanating from Badger, didn't appear to diminish Hazel's wonderful warmth. She prevailed, and they were to pack up and leave. When all was arranged Jandy suddenly objected.

'But what about the axolotls?' Hazel turned a look of amazement and muted fury on her. She had enough with Badger, without his blasted axolotls.

'It's okay – we'll stop off and leave a note for Lanky – he'll feed them,' said Badger.

So the two of them were bundled into the car with a couple of boxes of possessions, the axolotls fed and a note posted through another chalet letterbox, and off they drove, back to Moon Farm.

After they had driven in silence for about an hour Hebe said, 'Oh do let's go back the Farthingale way – I love to see the house rise up out of the corn.' Hazel turned from the wheel and flashed her a grateful smile – she was after all still loyally part of the household. Badger looked resentful, defeated. He would hardly chip out a sentence, even when spoken to. Hebe smiled in anticipation, hugging the fairytale to herself.

As they settled in Hazel would complain about Badger as soon as the two of them left the room. 'Did you see that? He's hostile and resentful. . .' suddenly beaming again when they came back, with the-show-must-go-smile. '*Here* they are. And what have you two been planning?' she asked indulgently.

Jandy couldn't cope with it, Hazel was the last person to be deceitful in the normal course of events. Shane when he was home was above it all, Nick locked in adolescent support of his sister and the Other Children, and against parents and their friends. When Lynnet came she briefly gave Badger her regal regard, and passed on to matters she found more worthy of her attention. Poor Badger, who actually loved Hebe, found himself wrong-footed at every turn. He said to Hebe, in the privacy of her bedroom, the door firmly shut against the rest of the household, 'Your female relations and their friends are all bitches, and if you stay here you'll get like them.'

Hazel turned to Jandy as her most ardent lieutenant to back her up where Badger was concerned. But Jandy was strangely recalcitrant. She said nothing but saw Hazel being as nice as sugar-pie to Badger. Aware that Hazel was attempting to encourage her to express Hazel's own hostility towards him, Jandy was suddenly awol.

Hazel burst out suddenly, passionately, in spite of her own suggestion that Badger move in, 'If Hebe had a father here to protect her there would be no question of Badger staying, it wouldn't arise. If Rex was here he wouldn't have it.' It was insufferable to her to have him in the house, but she was frightened of losing Hebe.

To compound Hazel's frustration, Hebe insisted on taking Badger on full view to Farthingale Fete. Jasper, captaining the Farthingale Eleven against Weston, won a goldfish, promptly named Maggie by the Barbers, after Mrs Thatcher, who now led the Tories.

'It's terrible, a poor dumb creature,' said Jandy, looking at the fish turning round in the jampot. 'And it's a disgrace, keeping it in that pot.'

'We're going to get her a lovely big bowl to splash about in, so you can just shut up Jandy. And if Mrs Thatcher was in charge of everything, we'd have some proper government,' said Margaret.

'Proper government – huh,' jeered Jandy.

'Proper government my eye,' scoffed Hazel. 'It's not likely to happen,' – they all agreed on that.

It was the year of the Queen's Jubilee, much in evidence. Hazel had a new jubilee tea tin with the Queen wreathed in flowers and smiles, admired by Jandy whilst making the tea. Hazel looked back at her in an odd way and said, 'Why shouldn't the Queen be celebrated, she's given years of loyal service.'

'Yes,' agreed Jandy. This infuriated Hazel, frustrated she couldn't argue against anything.

They watched the television news and Hazel poured scorn on the new Tory leader. 'That bloody woman. Doesn't she look absolutely vile in that dress?'

Everybody agreed with gusto, Nick said, 'They all look awful and the Queen looks pretty silly in that crown.'

'The Queen? The Queen looks very nice,' said an outraged Hazel. Nick looked amused, expecting a usual 'All this mimsying around in ermine' speech. 'They held this country together during the War,' Hazel said, choked. She turned a look of contempt on all of them, retreated into herself, said little the rest of the day.

Jandy's visit to Farthingale that summer was overshadowed, and started badly. She dismounted from the car, Alan unloaded her case, and they went through into the house. Margaret laying the table stopped to welcome them. The cat stretched and yawned and slowly came over to have her head rubbed. Jandy turned about, seeing the dog through the glass patio door and calling him.

'Oh my God. What happened?' The young Great Dane looked miserably through into the sitting room, raising his heavy head at the sound of his name – the head was swollen to about five times its usual size.

The Barbers were terribly upset. 'We don't know. Poor

Hector – he's a very sad dog, I'm afraid.'

When they saw Hazel she said, 'It's all this blasted crop spraying. Since Mr Harker died young Harker is going mad with the chemicals. There's another dog like it on the other side of the village.'

Farthingale and District Conservation Society convened in an emergency meeting and issued another public statement condemning the use of pesticides on crops, and when the Barbers went off to Dunwich for their holiday Dr Barber put poor Hector down.

Irritated by the way things were going in her household with Hebe and Badger, and by Jandy's withdrawal, Hazel vented her frustration by suddenly criticising her elderly female relations.

'They never married, they took no responsibility, they sponged off the family. The wives resented it, the way the unmarried sisters had to be looked after. They contributed nothing to the family but were a perpetual drain.'

'I thought they looked after you for two years when you were small and your mother was ill?'

'The Aunts! Those two. They were spinsters,' jeered Hazel.

Jandy had been in mental hospitals with spinsters and saw how they were made over into family scapegoats, how often they picked up the pieces after other people and took the brunt of any wild dislike that was around, because they had no one to defend them. Hazel's two aunts were long in their graves now but still apparently not free from contempt.

'I like spinsters.' It was one of those words, like fairies, that Jandy didn't have an inclination towards Hazel's views.

On her way to Moon Farm she had passed Tom Feetham working in Harker's fields. He lifted an arm and she called out a greeting. Tom was unmarried. He had nursed his mother until she died, then lived alone in the council bungalow with his dog. Clean and neat, he didn't bother with fancy clothes, although he had an old rocker's hank of hair falling at the front. Had he had a sweet on a girl at school who married someone else? What went through his mind on the two mile asthmatic crawl to Dr Barber in the night? More than anyone

Tom felt the way a leaf moves, he knew the land under his feet, he was one with the wordless yearnings, the mute suffering of animals. It was Tom who waded into a field in the pouring rain to retrieve Kitty-Kitty, the mother and granny of the farm cats, when he heard her cry. Lifting her from her kittens and cradling her under his donkey jacket out of the rain, he walked miles over fields to take her to Margaret. 'Look who I've found Margaret.'

'Oh Kitty!' She took the cat, frail from recently giving birth, who looked up at her, sighed, and died. 'She died in my arms. She was so weak.'

'What happened to the kittens?'

'Tom was so good, he went back and got them. But they died without their mother.'

There was respect between Tom and Jandy, especially since her journey through the fog with Rip, the Alsatian. She was never flippant with him. He knew the truth in the way animals behave, the delicacy, the withholding. But all she could do was to wave back to him across the corn, an exchange of goodwill.

'Why on earth are you crying?' asked Hazel, taken aback.

'I just am.'

The following summer was the first one Jandy had ever missed going to East Anglia. 'I'm not going,' she said to Andrew, whom she lived with but was about to leave. 'They can all get on without me, the whole lot of them. . .'

He laughed. He rather liked Hazel, thought her spirited but without rigour. Hazel said he was politically motivated, as though that was an accusation.

Adamant, she yet felt a twinge when she slapped idly through his *Guardian* and came across an ad. in the personal column. 'Looking for relatives of Grove or Acre in the Stockport area – contact Moon Farm, Coney Weston 392'.

Hazel must be lonely. She remembered a picnic from the year before, noisy and jubilant, Hebe had clenched her fist in the air and said, 'Granny power – ye-e-e-es!' Everyone had laughed, even Hazel. But no one saw when she turned to clear the picnic plates she had blinked away tears amongst these alien adults for whom she appeared to be responsible.

Suffering slight guilt feelings, Jandy wrote to Hazel in the early autumn, picturing Moon Farm among bare fields and plundered fruit trees.

Hazel Marlowe to Jandy Lockhart Moon Farm –
Hallowe'en

And may all your spells prosper!
Thank you for your long letter, the card and the lovely seal – which now lends its weight to the media as it hangs over the wall behind the telly. So you're no longer with Andrew. You sound to be enjoying your new room and its location. I hope the roofs and chimneypots are good to look at – they can be extremely satisfying. Hebe is thoroughly enjoying herself at Cambridge, she's taken to the social whirl like a duck to water. Badger has taken it badly and is his own worst enemy in the relationship. At the moment the engagement is ORF but Badger is still with us.

Shane goes his merry way – happy in his work and v. well content with Karin. Nick is working part-time at the pottery with Badger, and studying for his exams the rest of the time. And Lynnet, dear girl, has finally got O-level Maths. So she feels she can hold her head up with the rest of the family.

We enjoyed mid-Wales enormously. I was delighted with the variety. We had good weather, did a great mileage by car *and* on foot, and want to go back. Jo has a beautifully furnished guest house right by the sea. She looks well, has gained great confidence but is otherwise little changed. Billy is at Aberystwyth doing a second degree, finds it dull after Ruskin, and is v. politically active. He was badly beaten up by the police at the big demo outside Grunwicks. I think we all recharged our spiritual batteries among the heather and the cliffs.

I have finished the first draft of my book, and am going to have it typed professionally. Nick reckons it'll go like

176

hot cakes – Blimey I wish it would. Please don't tell Margaret I have mentioned it, but there is much Jasper trouble at the moment, re: motorbikes, friends, and trust. He is not working at school and wants to leave as soon as he possibly can, even though he's Head Boy! A. & M. seem scared of putting their feet down.

Are you ever coming this way again? I have been having some day-long migraine attacks – due to me age, no doubt. So I think a spot of meditation or sumpin' is called for. Dr Barber seems to have evolved a lifestyle in his bed, he's painting in oils and apparently confesses it's laziness which stops him getting up. But why not at his age I say! Must go. Write again.

Love from us all,
Hazel

The final eighteen months of Hazel's life were crowded with blows to her self-esteem.

Mr Harker, her elderly landlord, gallant and old-fashioned towards her when he visited, always spruce with a rosebud in his lapel, who would sit with a cup of tea and talk of the doings in Thankful and enquire about the children – died suddenly, and young Harker took over. Peremptory and abrasive, he sent her a stiff barely polite letter, demanding more money and alleging she was living at Moon Farm without paying a proper rent, and he wasn't a charity. Hazel dealt easily with this – a swift verbal blow back – 'I have paid every rent rise without demur, and if you wish to raise the rent perhaps you would like to approach me in a proper manner.' Yet it shook her confidence.

To demonstrate the full extent of his hostility, young Harker sent a plane over one Saturday morning to crop spray, and Moon Farm was deluged by a hail of chemicals, the plane zooming low over the house repeatedly in a menacing manner, making a deliberate attack on the house and garden, for the fields were obviously separate. All the windows shook, the glass was covered in chemicals so she and Nick couldn't see out, hail beat on the roof, imprisoning the occupants in the house in its vapours. Livid, she went straight to the telephone and called the police, lodging an official complaint. But it had happened, and nobody could do anything about that.

At school, where she had been Acting Headmistress for months, another teacher was appointed Head in her place. She applied to another school, but didn't get the appointment. 'At one level, I don't care, but I wouldn't have minded a potty little headship,' she confided to Margaret regretfully.

Then there was the almighty row with Rex over Nick's teenage friendship with Juliet, one of Gillian's children. Rex came to visit with thunder and an ultimatum.

'He is to stop ringing her immediately, because it's completely inappropriate, they are half-brother and sister. And more particularly because I'm paying for both lots of telephone calls,' he raged. Nick answered fury with fury, and when they visited Lynnet and Jandy fell about laughing, but Hazel was devastated. She saw it as a slight to her children.

'Oh my children don't count, Nick doesn't exist as far as Rex is concerned.' She became speechless with grief, her face full of pain.

All in all, she felt jostled and intimidated, felt alone in a way she never did before when the children were small, because she had had them to protect.

The next time Jandy went there Moon Farm was surrounded by uncut corn, the house run by resentful adolescents, and Hazel was unwell with a sickness which seemed both mental and physical. Visitors in and out of the house had to pass Hebe and Nick and Badger, who formed a teenage knot about Badger's motorbike, talking amongst themselves and silent and suspicious of everybody else. Once inside, Hazel ran through a catalogue of Badger's shortcomings – he was trying to prevent Hebe from going back to Cambridge, he wouldn't allow her out without him, he was difficult about his meals, he was living there rent-free. When the three came through the door Hazel was bright and friendly with them, as though

178

nothing was wrong.

Shane was away at Rex's, Paul and Dale Perkyn and entourage had finally left the area. Margaret was busy nursing her father-in-law, who had been diagnosed with a terminal illness. So Hazel was unwell and convalescent all that summer, sitting in an armchair looking out onto the garden, at the buddleia and butterflies the golden rod, the Suffolk sky – smelling an apple she could no longer face eating.

Ill with a strange sickness, she didn't want either Lynnet or Jandy in the house for long, disturbing the quiet. Lynnet had split with her husband and taken their small child, and Jandy had walked out on the man she lived with and gone careening after somebody else, and Hazel felt she had no point of contact with either of them, their way of being adult was alien and seemed to her to be part of a huge irresponsibility.

At Windy Ridge Dr Barber died. It had been expected but the Barbers were distraught. 'We're going to miss him terribly,' said Alan. It was a hot but gloomy summer in Farthingale that year, with Hazel unwell, and the Barbers preparing for a funeral. Mrs Thatcher had won the General Election.

'Can you collect Jandy at five o'clock?' Hazel said before Margaret left.

'This is going to take a long time,' she said despondently, as Jandy settled into a chair.

'What do you think is wrong with you?'

Hazel sighed. 'Ohhhhhhh. Over twenty years of bringing up children alone. I'm exhausted. Totally exhausted. It's going to take a long long time,' she said hopelessly.

At Windy Ridge it was a time of low voices and of sitting around between endless cups of tea. On the table were a pile of photos of Dr. Barber at various times in his life, one propped up showed a four-year-old hugging a big bear cub, looking out at the camera, towards his life and the future, with confidence. He and the cub stand between artistic sister who became successful, and baby brother who was to be slaughtered in the Great War. The cub with impenetrable gaze, bereft of its mother, seeming at ease with the children.

His watercolours, framed in passe-partout, surrounded them

179

on the walls, small glimpses of Italy – gardens with bourgainvillea, wild land and olives in the wind, palm trees and sea and mediterranean high colour. A big watercolour of an English river with many greens of trees and grass and silver swaying leaves. Dominating the wall a large early painting of his art teacher's room in Paris – overwhelming deep blue, a grand piano, a bowl of pink and dusky flowers – the blooms of summer 1913; a breeze moves the gauze at the window. The delight of the painter is stroked into the tranquillity, and to those left behind it seemed he had finally walked back into this blue room of his youth, the curtains move in the breeze at his passing. As a young man he had sat in this room dreaming of being an artist and the dream followed him throughout his life, giving him pleasure rather than regret. They remembered how his doctor's fingers often moved as he sat, as though hearing and following invisible melodies.

The notice in St. Edfric's Free Press read 'Theodore Marie Barber, doctor of medicine, served in the Artists' Rifles in the First World War, peacefully at home aged 84.'

The next time Jandy went to Moon Farm it was arranged that she would return to look after Hazel, when the children had gone back to university. Hazel concurred in this, and didn't move from her chair in front of the window, was subdued, spoke quietly and only wanted Jandy there for a couple of hours.

Then she railed against Rex and against her life with him. 'Look at all the lives that one man has ruined. His children's lives. Gillian's – Gillian's life has been appalling with him, she's at the end of her tether. Eve's. That's his secretary. He's led everybody a dance. One man – and so much destruction.'

'I don't see that he has wrecked their lives,' replied Jandy evenly.

'Oh well, if you can't see it, there's nothing more to be said. Love is destructive,' she averred.

'Why?' she pleaded, looking hopelessly at the garden, the lawn, the golden rod, 'why does love always have to include hate? Why?'

'Does it always?' replied Jandy in a low voice, wary of upsetting illness.

'Sexual love does,' Hazel responded definitely. 'It most certainly does. Is there any need for it? Love doesn't have to be that way. The way a mother loves doesn't include hatred. . .'

Something dormant and intransigent awoke in Jandy and in spite of her intention she replied, '*No*. The way a mother loves wants to dominate. . .'

Hazel looked upwards, as though disengaging herself, and gave a great sigh, slow and despairing, and looked away. But not before their eyes met in frank momentary hostility. They talked then of other things.

'See you soon in September then,' said Jandy as she heard Margaret's car. 'Everything will be fine – you'll see. You need to rest and recover and not worry about a thing.'

Hazel went back to smelling her apple, her body already turning to a husk, looking out onto the garden and the circle of gold. And that was the last image Jandy had of her.

She met Lynnet on the way in as she was on the way out, and they exchanged a few words in Moon Farm kitchen, boxes of Complan standing around the well-loved place.

'How is she?' For a second or two time seemed to have backtracked years, the children small and together with Hazel all prostrate upstairs with the 'flu. Jandy had taken up their meals and fetched the trays down again, opened the backdoor wide to let the air circulate, and exchanged brief words with Lynnet, newly arrived from school to take over the nursing. 'How is she?'

Lynnet was staying now at Oaktree Farm, a couple of miles away, for Hazel couldn't bear to have either Lynnet or Jandy in the house for long, braying with laughter at everything and imposing their own adult lives.

Hazel acquired from the doctor's fatal diagnosis the authority at Moon Farm she had lost. She left her chair and went through into the dining room. 'When you've finished tea I want to speak to you two alone in the other room, and Badger must pack his bags and leave by tomorrow morning,' she decreed, ignoring the murderous looks and going from the room.

As the summer and Hazel's life drew to its close she was locked in a view of it as a tragedy, with a villain – Rex – and an impetus which was irresistibly pulling her down into a spiral of despair. Pulling off her wedding ring she said to her children: 'You can sell this now,' over-dramatic and weary, dwelling inside her own drama for the last two or three years had drained her. On the day her lost baby was born Hazel died.

Lynnet drove Jandy to Diss, to see Hazel. A bright day of early autumn, September. Hazel in a coffin, her face yellow and bloated. Afterwards they went to the mere, sat talking and dabbling their bare feet in the water. 'Eeeeeeeeok,' shrieked Lynnet suddenly, as though she was her old self, as a fish swam close and nibbled her toes. 'They've got piranhas here now.' They collapsed into laughter, in spite of a gnawing in the stomach.

'They rang through when we were on holiday at Tintagel – we were trying to make a go of the marriage again,' said Lynnet, still trailing her toes. 'They told Jonathan. He didn't tell me until the evening. We were walking along the old path into the sea, that once led to Lyonesse, and then he told me. I had hysterics, I screamed at him – "Why didn't you tell me before?" and he said, "There's nothing that can be done, it's too late, and I wanted us to have one last day together." So we went back to Moon Farm the next day, but she didn't want me to stay there.'

'No, she didn't want me there for long either. I was expecting to come back to look after her, and I only got told because I happened to ring – there was nobody in the telephone box so I went in and rang Margaret and Alan. We chatted and then I asked how Hazel was, expecting to hear something quite ordinary and he said, "Oh it's very near the end." And Margaret said, "Well I thought I had let you know without actually saying it." So I said, "And how did you do that?" So she said, "Well Hazel asked me not to tell anybody, so I *conveyed* it without putting it into words." '

'Yes well, they can be peculiar, those two.'

'I'll say they can.' They talked on, aware that Hazel hadn't wanted either of them at Moon Farm near the end.

At night Jandy viewed the harvest moon, big and bloated and yellow. 'Oh Hazel, Hazel,' she spoke to it with aching heart.

Lynnet rang Rex urgently that night. 'I think it's better if you don't come to the funeral.'

He sighed. 'Right. I would like to be there, but if it's going to cause trouble. . . we'll leave it.'

Everyone drove out for miles to a cursory silent disappearance of coffin, without flowers or hymns or words. The Barbers seemed the only true adults there. The relations hadn't come from Manchester, old Mrs Grove was too distraught at the suddenness of it. Afterwards, on Hazel's instruction, the four Marlowe children drove off to visit Thelnetham churchyard, where somewhere the dead baby lay, their brother.

'Yes, I think at the end Hazel thought of all her babies,' said Alan, quite broken at the sudden turn of events.

'Hazel seemed so strong,' said Margaret, 'yet anything could hurt her. It could be news about someone she didn't know on the other side of the world, or even some unhappy thing from hundreds of years ago – it could cut her to the bone.' She shook her head. 'Poor Hazel.'

'It's all wrong,' said Alan. 'She was so full of life.'

'Do you think she knew?' asked Jandy.

'No. She didn't know. She was exhausted all summer – the heat wearied her – but. . . I think she must have wondered. No – I'm sure she didn't know,'decided Margaret.

The doorbell rang and Mr Chew the greengrocer came into the kitchen with the order from his van. 'You're back, then.'

'Yes, we've just come from Mrs Marlowe's funeral.'

'Oh-ho, not much in common there,' observed Mr Chew, putting the box of vegetables on the kitchen table and taking out his order book. 'I mean – politics?'

'No – er – no – but. . . we had known her a very long time and she was our. . . she was. . . she was our very dearest friend,' said Alan.

At Thelnetham churchyard the four of them gazed about and saw the lychgate, and the oak where Hebe had used to drop her letters to the Fairy Queen. It was covered in ivy and grey with age, shadows lay across the grass, the dead baby was here, no one quite knew where.

'Look!' cried Hebe. 'Seven for a secret,' – she pointed at the sky, 'One-two-three-four-five-six-seven,' she counted out where seven blue-jays were whirling around in a spin of wings. 'Seven for a secret never to be told.'

Lynnet remembered after the baby was born and died. Withy House silent; something most terrible had happened. Her Mother and Daddy – not Hazel and Rex then – were distant, unspeaking. Oppression lay in the house and in the marriage. Years later Rex told her he had wrapped the baby in his shawl, and kissed him and held him. Then he laid him in a cardboard shoebox and – an atheist – had crept out alone at night to bury him in hallowed ground.

At Windy Ridge Margaret busied herself preparing tea, for the young Marlowes were coming from Thelnetham. Jandy thought of the day when she had first met them, Hebe a tiny newborn baby in the pram the sunshine full on her, Knettishall Heath swarming with summer people, and three year old Shane running joyfully around without his clothes, until he was caught and with laughter put into trunks, to bathe in the river. Withy House, Hazel and Rex as she had first known them, the dark rooms, the chill part of the house, Hazel's voice offering her a job – 'Looking after Baby – nice family – pleasant house – as many books to read as you want. . .' her hand lightly round Jandy's shoulder she had looked at Rex, who was looking intently at Jandy. She had a strange feeling of being captured by the splendid glittering couple, a match for everyone in their orbit. Hazel – small, slim, dominant. She held a cigarette high just away from her face and sent a blue challenging look out to Rex. They knew who they were, they were decisive, they had fought and survived a war and were rearing a family of golden ones.

Margaret came in bearing cups, and they had some desultory chat.

Banned from the funeral, a gaunt Rex took himself off to his study, to drink. Different and disjointed images of her swam before him and tormented him. Hazel as he had first seen her, with a group of friends, wearing a hand-knitted jumper, on leave from college. They shared the darkness, listening to the 'Warsaw Concerto' on the wireless, the piano crashed down laden with meaning for them. He was to return to ship soon, she was to go back to college. Then her face when she found out about Liesl – amazed and hurt; scornful at Gillian and the others; amused when she heard about Eve. He had thought then that maybe she was at last taking on board the reality of an adult male's life. Then out of his drinking her face appeared smug under a terrible hat at Lynnet's wedding. Haggard at the hospital bedside of Shane. He had tried to explain to her about Liesl – how for him this poor broken girl was part of what as a teenager he had been fighting the War for; how her pitiful state reached deep inside him and affected him as a man. And Hazel had listened, wanting to understand, sympathetic.

After that happened, they moved downward, into East Anglia. It was a good time. He felt incredibly tender towards her, she was strong in spirit yet looked frail with the burden of their child in her body. . . They had wandered through the churchyard hand in hand, picking the baby's name from the tombs – Simon or Sarah. Back home she made a meal and he trimmed the wicks on the red shaded paraffin lamps and wrote 'Our civilisation recognises the dominance of the weak – the defenceless Child is supreme, we guard its rights fiercely we defend it, for humanity itself is the Divine Child.'

185

*   *   *   *

Margaret and Jandy went over the silent house – Hazel's bedroom with her desk and pens and manuscripts; the charcoal picture of the young poet Rex on the wall. On the mantel a picture from the *Book of Hours* showing a mediaeval summer with hot blue sky and brilliant greenery, and a photo of ten year old Shane laughing at a parrot on his arm.

Outside crusted at the top of the bedroom window empty mud nests, awaiting the birds' return – their cries and twitterings part of the children's bedtimes and risings. But they never came back. On a high chest sat the musical box, banished to the landing now, wound up it began to tinkle out 'Boys and Girls come out to play The moon doth shine as bright as day. . .' Outside lay the smoking dark sky of autumn; inside the ghostly children's voices galloping, scrying, and slowly winding down.

As though they couldn't bear to be in the house any longer without Hazel, the young Marlowes packed up and left Moon Farm within weeks of her death.

'Poor little cat. I found her on the front windowsill there, she was so pleased to see somebody, I expect she's wondering where all the children have gone,' said Margaret, letting the little tabby cat down onto the floor.

'No, now darling, I'm putting my foot down about this. I said that before, I know, but I mean it this time. Why didn't those children take the cat?' said Alan forcefully.

'Oh darling, I don't know, do I? They're young, they don't think.'

'We're becoming a cats and dogs home for the animals of irresponsible people. There's Susan and there's your mother's dog. . .'

Hearing her name, the little white cat that Jandy had dumped on them tripped into the room with expectant face.

'It's all right, my Sue, Alan doesn't mean it.'

'No, I don't mind Susan. . .'

186

'Well Mother was hardly irresponsible by dying,' Margaret pointed out evenly.

'Oh darling, oh I didn't mean such a thing,' he said contritely.

Perceiving things were going well, Margaret said nothing and bided her time.

'That's a nice little cat, I'm not going to see her just dumped like that,' she said to Madeleine.

She remembered the first time she had seen the cat, old Mrs Grove saying warmly, 'Oh a tabby kitten – I love a tabby cat, we always had one at home, we had a lovely one, before the War – the first war I mean – Chilperry – now why was he called that. . ?

'Rex got very demanding,' Lynnet confided to Jandy three years later, over the post-Christmas Baileys. 'He was like a small child, he had to be talked to all the time. I was nearly eight months with Louise and was lugging myself round the house, and he wouldn't even let me go to the loo, he came and shouted outside the door, "What do you think about Mrs Thatcher doing so and so – what about that then?" In desperation I shrieked, "Rex go and put the kettle on and I'll be down in a minute and make us some coffee." '

Defiant to the last, he rowed frequently with his long-term girlfriend Eve, and argued with the doctor when told he must give up alcohol. 'Oh I've been told by a higher authority than *you* I must give up drinking' – the doctor bridled somewhat at this, for what possible higher authority could there be? '*I've* been told by West Sussex county Magistrates' court I must give up drinking,' he finished triumphantly.

Rex, at fifty-six worn out with rowing and writing and drinking, plagued by ill-health and alcoholism, finished the last page of what he knew would be his last book. Bound to the faerie England of Elizabeth he took his leave in hose and ruff as Elizabethan ghost: 'Ladies and gentlemen, my story ends. I hope I have not encroached too much on your time, and that all will be well. And so give you good night.'

'He didn't like to let you out of his sight,' said Lynnet, 'he wanted to do as much talking as possible, he was waiting for the operation, but he died on the operating table, before I had the baby.'

They sipped, each thinking of the couple who had been so important in their lives.

'When I heard I didn't believe it, I didn't believe somebody as alive as Rex could die,' said Jandy simply.

Preparing for the concert in the Abbey, Alan polished his shoes and brushed his suit, and carefully put the mayoral chain of office over his head. He smoothed his spruce goatee beard. With his almond eyes and acquiline nose, the effect was rather Angevin. He took two pinches of snuff, and sneezed into a big white handkerchief. Then he loaded the wheelchair into the boot of the car, and went to fetch Margaret.

That same day in his Lancashire home town, Harry Blumenthal also put on his mayoral chain. He was going to open a drop-in and welfare centre for former miners – a project which had his whole-hearted support. He had backed the NUM during the bad year of '84 and the sub-committee of which he had been chairman then had voted through free meals for striking miners' children. The clasps of his chain were made from Welsh gold, mined specially by members of the NUM.

The Barbers drove through a June vista of corn and sky, and they reached town in good time. 'I should have thought,' said Margaret querulously, 'after all that fuss over the hanging baskets, they might have cleaned the graffiti.' On the wall facing the carpark were enormous painted letters from the year before – the Poll Tax year, the citizens once again revolting. ST. EDFRIC'S SAYS NO – rather a muted response compared to 1381, when the Abbey was torched.

Alan assisted Margaret into the wheelchair and Jandy wandered along with the bags. At the Abbey entrance they were issued with programmes, fronted by a quote from Magna Carta in a scrolled box: 'No free man shall be seized or imprisoned, or dispossessed, or outlawed, or in any way brought to ruin; we will not go against any man nor send against him, save by legal judgment of his peers or by the law of the land.'

The Abbey was already packed and people were filing in all the time. The displays of flowers sumptuous, jewelled lights cast down upon all. Helen Grove had driven down from Manchester, with Lynnet and children. Michael and Madeleine were near the front, and Jon and Romaine Warrender. Madeleine helped Margaret off with her jacket and as she turned she caught sight of Nick, and then Hebe. 'Look darling,' she said to Alan. 'And Shane's come too – over there.' He was with a tall woman. 'That must be Nancy,' she whispered, and they all leaned forward to get a glimpse of his American wife.

Helen was looking through the programme and eating humbugs, and Lynnet gazed round, thinking of her schooldays and the statue of the unchanging boy-king, with his pudding-basin haircut. She pointed him out to her daughters, and waved to Jandy across the rows of people. The Abbey was full already.

Jandy, wedged into her seat, thought of Hazel. 'Hello dear – what a treat you're about to have,' she would have said. And Rex spoke to her from the dead and his book. 'Strip, child – strip – give a few thousand brain cells in solution a treat. Yes, I died. I have no body. But the mind can hold on to what it has enjoyed. You'd be surprised. . .' She looked for the shape of the crescent, as he had shown her, but the floor wasn't visible because of the constant push of people coming up from the great studded door. But she had no doubt it was there, in place. All things were in place. The crescent, the cross, and the star of David, all under the Eye of God.

There was a murmur among the gathering – Yehudi Menuhin had just been glimpsed. The procession at the back was forming, in preparation for its journey up the aisle with brass Cross and white-frilled choir-boys. The organ suddenly filled the great Abbey with its roar.

Alan thought of Hazel, how she would have loved to have been here. He saw her very specifically in a light blouse, her hair loose, as she had looked when Rex and himself – just the

189

three of them in those days – had driven one day out to the sea, over the flat land, past the slightly moving windmills – a wonder to them all, they slowed the car down each time they passed the clattering creaking things.

Once on the beach she had unpacked rum-laced coffee in a thermos, and told of when she had gone to hear Menuhin play in Manchester just after the War. Her eyes alight, her face keen. Then she unpacked the sandwiches she had made and they all tucked into them, their faces reflected by the bright sea.

And that's how Rex too, drinking alone on the day of Hazel's funeral, had thought of her. And of the day of their wedding. How he had kept running his fingers between neck and collar. Having no demob suit as yet, the borrowed clothes were tight in places. And then the sudden cloud of confetti which they delightedly tried to dodge. When they were in the train he recalled Hazel turning to him and throwing her arms round his neck, passionate and enthusiastic all at once. Then she had unpinned her hat, as though she knew how much it had irked him, and when he said 'I've been wanting to do that all morning' she had laughed back at him, her eyes refracting blue light, and she had taken the hat and thrown it joyously from the train as it started moving, back at the relations, who stood together in a line in their best clothes, waving.

She was such a fine girl. She could fight her corner, she could be steel when needed. She stuck up for what she believed in. And afterwards, when the babies started coming, all her care was for them. With a twist in his heart he thought of their wedding joy, when they linked hands and ran through confetti, their hearts high, and with so many plans, bursting to begin their life together in the newly free land.

'And we fairies, that do run
  By the triple Hecate's team,
From the presence of the sun,
  Following darkness like a dream,
Now are frolic; not a mouse
  Shall disturb this hallow'd house.'

from *A Midsummer Night's Dream*
William Shakespeare